“It’

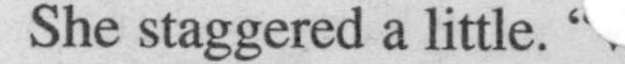

She staggered a little. “

“You. On the beach. Three years ago.”

She blinked up at him, rubbed her fingertips across her mouth and then drew in a long, shaky breath. “Congratulations,” she said at last. “Finally you remembered.”

“You knew?” he demanded, bracing his legs wide apart as he folded his arms over his chest. “You remembered and didn’t say anything to me?”

“Why would I?” she asked, gathering up the fabric she’d dropped when he was kissing her. “You think I’m *proud* of that night?”

“You ought to be,” he told her sharply, “we were great together.”

“We were strangers. It was a huge mistake.”

Dear Reader,

Thanks to all of the letters I received asking for more KINGS OF CALIFORNIA books, I'm happy to offer you the first book in a new Kings miniseries—with more to come, I promise!

Conquering King's Heart is about Jesse King, a former world champion surfer. Jesse is the youngest of four brothers, and in the next two months you'll be seeing more of them, as well.

But for now, let's talk about Jesse. He's traveled all over the world, living life his way. Now he's retired from competition and has settled down in Morgan Beach—a place that haunts his memory thanks to the "mystery woman" he met one night three years ago.

Bella Cruz is that mystery woman, and she's not happy that Jesse has moved into her hometown, changing everything she loves about the place.

When these two meet again, the fireworks are well worth watching!

The KINGS OF CALIFORNIA will continue in the next two months with stories about Jesse's brothers Justice and Jefferson. Then of course, there's still Jericho to be heard from.

I hope you have as much fun reading this story as I did writing it. I love hearing from my readers! E-mail me at maureenc@maureenchild.com or send snail mail to P.O. Box 1883, Westminster, CA 92684-1883.

And please visit my Web site at www.maureenchild.com.

Until then, happy reading!

Maureen

MAUREEN CHILD

CONQUERING KING'S HEART

Silhouette® Desire

Published by Silhouette Books
America's Publisher of Contemporary Romance

ISBN-13: 978-0-373-76965-0

CONQUERING KING'S HEART

This edition published by arrangement with Harlequin Books S.A.

Visit Silhouette Books at www.eHarlequin.com

Printed in U.S.A.

Books by Maureen Child

Silhouette Desire

**Expecting Lonergan's Baby* #1719
**Strictly Longergan's Business* #1724
**Satisfying Lonergan's Honor* #1730
The Part-Time Wife #1755
Beyond the Boardroom #1765
Thirty Day Affair #1785
†*Scorned by the Boss* #1816
†*Seduced by the Rich Man* #1820
†*Captured by the Billionaire* #1826
††*Bargaining for King's Baby* #1857
††*Marrying for King's Millions* #1862
††*Falling for King's Fortune* #1868
High-Society Secret Pregnancy #1879
Baby Bonanza #1893
An Officer and a Millionaire #1915
Seduced Into a Paper Marriage #1946
††*Conquering King's Heart* #1965

Silhouette Nocturne

‡*Eternally* #4
‡*Nevermore* #10
‡*Vanished* #57

*Summer of Secrets
‡The Guardians
†Reasons for Revenge
††Kings of California

MAUREEN CHILD

is a California native who loves to travel. Every chance they get, she and her husband are taking off on another research trip. The author of more than sixty books, Maureen loves a happy ending and still swears that she has the best job in the world. She lives in Southern California with her husband, two children and a golden retriever with delusions of grandeur. Visit Maureen's Web site at www.maureenchild.com.

To Patti Canterbury Hambleton.
For years of friendship and laughter.
For shared memories and too many adventures to count.
For always being a touchstone in my life.
I love you.

One

Jesse King loved women.

And they loved him right back.

Well, all except one.

Jesse walked into Bella's Beachwear and stopped just inside the store. His gaze wandered the well-kept if decrepit building and he shook his head at the stubbornness of women.

Hard to believe that Bella Cruz preferred this ramshackle building to what he was offering. He'd arrived in Morgan Beach, a tiny coastal town in southern California, nine months ago. He'd bought up several of the run-down, eclectic shops on Main Street, rehabbed some, razed others, then built the kind of stores and offices that would actually *attract* shoppers to the downtown district.

Everyone had been happy to sign on the dotted line. They'd accepted his buyout offers with barely disguised glee and most of them were now renting retail space from him. But not Bella Cruz. Oh, no. This woman had been working against him for months.

She'd spearheaded a sit-in campaign, getting a few of her friends to plant themselves in front of his bull-dozers for an afternoon. She'd held a protest march down Main Street that consisted of Bella herself, four women, two kids and a three-legged dog. And finally, she'd resorted to trying to pull off a candlelight vigil in memory of the "historic" buildings of Morgan Beach.

There had been five people standing outside his of-fice holding candles the night the first big summer storm had blown in. Within minutes, they were all drenched, the candle flames drowned out. Bella was the only one left standing in the dark, glaring up at him as he looked at her through his office window.

"Why is she taking this all so personally?" he won-dered. It wasn't as if he'd come to town to deliberately ruin her life.

He'd come here for the waves.

When professional surfers stopped riding competi-tively, they settled in a place where they could always find a good ride year-round. Most ended up in Hawaii, but, as a native Californian, Jesse had decided on Morgan Beach. His whole family still lived in the state and Morgan was close enough that he could keep in touch and far enough away from his three brothers that he wouldn't trip on them with every step. He liked his family. A lot. That didn't mean he wanted to live right on top of them.

So he was building himself a little kingdom here in this small town and the only thing keeping it from being absolutely perfect was Bella Cruz.

"The evil landlord stops by to gloat," a low, female voice said from somewhere nearby.

He turned around and spotted his nemesis, crouched behind the counter, rearranging a display of sunglasses, flip-flops and tote bags. Her dark brown eyes were fixed on him with the steely look of a woman about to spray a roach with Raid.

"You're not armed, are you?" he asked, walking toward her slowly. "Because you look as if you'd like to put me out of my misery."

"Out of *my* misery is more like it," she answered wryly. Then she stood up and Jesse took in her latest outfit.

Bella stood about five foot eight, which was good, because he liked his women tall enough that he didn't get a crick in his neck when he kissed them. Not that he was thinking about kissing Bella. It was just an observation.

She had wavy black hair that fell to the middle of her back, huge chocolate eyes and a lusciously full mouth he had yet to see curved into a smile. Pretty, he thought. Except for the clothes.

Every time he saw her she looked as if she were about to pose for the cover of *Amish Monthly*: loose-fitting cotton tops and full, floor-length skirts. Probably just as well, he told himself. He liked his women curvy and by the look of her, she had all the curves of a box. Seemed strange to him, though, that a woman who made her living designing and selling women's swimwear looked as if she'd never worn one of her own garments.

"What do you want, Mr. King?"

He grinned deliberately. He knew the power of that smile. Enough women over the years had told him just what his dimples did to their knees. Bella's knees appeared to be rock solid. Oh, well. He wasn't interested in seducing her anyway. Or so he kept reminding himself.

"I wanted to tell you that we're going to start rehabbing this building next month."

"Rehabbing," she repeated and screwed up her face as if even the word itself were distasteful. "You mean knocking down the walls? Tearing up the hardwood floor? Getting rid of the leaded windows? That kind of rehabbing?"

He shook his head. "What is it exactly, that you have against well-insulated buildings and sound roofs?"

She crossed her arms under her breasts and Jesse was distracted for a moment. Apparently, she did have at least *one* good set of curves.

"My roof doesn't leak," she told him. "Robert Towner was an excellent landlord."

"Yes, so I've heard," he said with a sigh. "Repeatedly."

"You could take lessons from him."

"He didn't even bother to repaint the outside of your shop," Jesse pointed out.

"Why would he do that?" she demanded. "I painted it myself three years ago."

His mind boggled. "You actually *chose* to paint your business purple? On purpose?"

"It's lavender."

"Purple."

She inhaled sharply and gave him another glare that should have set his hair on fire. But Jesse was made of sterner stuff. He was a King. And Kings didn't cave for anybody.

"You won't be happy until every building on Main Street is beige with rust-colored trim, will you?" Shaking her head, she gave him a pitying look now, but it was wasted on Jesse. Kings didn't need anyone's pity. "We're all going to be Stepfords. Will we all march in lockstep, do you think? Dress alike?"

"Please God, no," he said, with a glance at her ensemble.

She colored briefly. "*My point is,* there's no individuality here anymore. Morgan Beach used to have personality."

"And wood rot."

"It was eclectic."

"Shabby."

"You're nothing but a corporate robot," she accused.

Jesse was stunned that anyone would describe him that way. He'd never set out to be a corporate anything. Hell, he'd gone out of his way to avoid the trap that all Kings eventually landed in. The business world. In fact, the King name had been a pain in his ass for most of his life.

His father, brothers, cousins—all Kings everywhere—seemed to be locked into offices. Didn't matter to Jesse if those offices were luxurious penthouse suites. He'd never wanted anything to do with that world.

He'd watched his three older brothers slide into the family business concerns as if they'd been molded for the task. Even Justice, on his ranch, was a businessman first and foremost. But Jesse had broken away. Become a professional surfer and damn if he hadn't loved the life. While his brothers and cousins were wearing suits and running meetings, he was traveling the world, looking for the perfect ride. He did things his way. Lived his life the way he wanted to. He didn't answer to anyone.

Until his favorite surfboard maker went out of business a few years ago. Jesse had bought up the company because he wanted access to the boards he favored. He'd done the same thing when he'd found the perfect wet suit. And the ideal swim trunks. Pretty soon, he'd actually done what he'd always insisted he wouldn't. Become a businessman. Not just a drone, either—the head of King Beach, a giant, diversified company that centered around life on the beach. Ironic that the thing he loved had eventually turned him into what he'd never wanted to be.

"Look," he said quietly, shaking away thoughts that were too troubling to focus on. "We don't have to be enemies."

"Oh, yes, we do."

Damn, she was stubborn. For ten years, he'd been at the top of his sport. He'd won hundreds of competitions, been featured in magazine ads, partied with the most glamorous celebrities and last year had even been named California's Sexiest Bachelor. He had money, charm and all the women he could possibly want. So why was he torturing himself by standing here listening to Bella Cruz harp at him?

Because she intrigued him. Whether it was her obvious enmity for him, or her sheer hardheadedness, he wasn't sure. But there was something about Bella that got to him. Felt somehow…familiar.

Jesse pulled in a deep breath, leaned both hands on the counter and looked at her. "It's just some walls and windows, Ms. Cruz—or can I call you Bella?"

"No, you cannot, and it's not just walls and windows." She held out her arms as if physically trying to hug the ratty old building. "This place has a history. The whole town did. Until *you* showed up, that is."

She gave him a look that was heat and ice both at the same time. Impressive. She was practically vibrating with banked rage. He'd always found a way around a woman's temper. Until now.

For months, he'd been trying to worm his way into her good graces. It would have made life easier if she'd agreed to an easy working relationship. She had friends in Morgan Beach. She was successful—in her own, cottage-industry kind of way. And dammit, women *liked* Jesse King.

"The town's history is still here," Jesse told her, "along with buildings that won't collapse at the first sign of a stiff breeze."

"Yeah," she muttered, "you're a real humanitarian."

He laughed. "I'm just trying to run a business," he said and nearly winced at the words. When had he become his brothers? His father?

"No, you're trying to run *my* business."

"Trust me when I say I have zero interest in your company." Jesse glanced behind her to where one of her custom-designed swimsuits was tacked to the wall.

Jesse's company catered to men. He knew what a guy was looking for in a wet suit, bathing suit or whatever. He had no idea what women were looking for and wouldn't expand until he knew. Though his stockholders and managers were after him to expand to women's gear, Jesse was standing firm against them. He had no idea what to stock for women, yet; he'd rather focus on what he did best. Bella Cruz could *have* the female share of the market.

"Then why are you here?" she asked, and he heard the toe of her shoe tapping against the floor. "My rent's not due for another three weeks."

"So warm. So welcoming," he said, giving Bella another smile. It bounced off her like bullets off a tank. Woman was determined to hate him. Jesse shoved his hands into the pockets of his khaki slacks and walked off to study the racks.

"I'm very welcoming. To customers," she said.

"Yeah, the store's so packed I can hardly walk."

She huffed out a breath. "Summer's over. Sales slow down a little."

"Funny, everyone else says business is great."

"Worried about your rent?" she asked.

"Should I be?"

"No," Bella said quickly. "I have a small, but loyal clientele."

"Uh-huh."

"You're impossible," he thought he heard her mutter. Jesse smiled to himself. Good to know he was getting to her as thoroughly as she was getting to him.

Beyond the plate-glass window, Morgan Beach was going about its day. It was late morning and the surfers were packing it in for the day. He knew all too well that the best rides were just after dawn, before the water was crowded with kids and moms and wannabes with their little belly boards.

People were wandering the tidy sidewalks, sitting at sidewalk cafés and, in general, enjoying the day. While he was standing in a women's-wear shop talking to a female who practically hissed when she saw him. Jesse stifled a sigh of impatience.

He shifted his gaze to the interior of Bella's place. Pale, cream-colored walls were dotted with handmade swimsuits tacked up beside framed posters of some of the best beaches in the world. And Jesse should know. He'd surfed most of those beaches. For ten years, he'd hardly been out of the water. He'd snatched up trophies, endorsement deals, nice fat checks and plenty of attention from the surf bunnies who followed the circuit.

Sometimes he really missed that life. Like now, for instance.

"So, since I'm your landlord, why don't we play nice?"

"You're only my landlord because Robert Towner's kids sold you the building after he died. He promised me that they wouldn't, you know," she said, regret tingeing her voice. "He promised that I could stay here another five years."

"But that wasn't in his will," Jesse reminded her as he turned around to meet her hard gaze. "His kids decided to sell. Hardly my fault."

"Of course it was your fault—you offered them a small fortune for the building!"

He smiled. "Good business."

Bella smothered a sigh. What good would it do? Facts were facts and the fact was, Jesse King was now the owner of her building, despite Robert's promises.

Robert Towner had been a sweet old man, a surrogate grandfather to Bella. They'd had coffee every morning, dinner at least once a week. She'd seen him far more often than his own children had and she'd hoped to actually buy the building from him one day. Unfortunately, Robert had died in a car accident nearly a year ago. Despite his assurances, he hadn't made any provisions for Bella in his will.

A month or so after Robert's death, his children sold the building to Jesse King and Bella had been worried about her future ever since. Robert had always kept the rent low enough so she could afford this great location. But she knew that Jesse King wouldn't be doing the same.

He was making "improvements" right and left and

would soon be raising the rents to pay for them. Which meant that Bella would have to look for another shop to rent. She'd have to leave Main Street and relocate farther inland, losing at least a quarter of her business, since many of her customers were drop-ins off the beach.

Jesse King was going to ruin everything. Just as he had three years ago.

Not that he remembered. The bastard.

Bella really wanted to kick something. Preferably her new landlord. Which was so far out of her character, she blamed that notion on him, too. Jesse King was the kind of man who expected the world to roll over and beg whenever he crooked his finger. The trouble was, it usually did.

He looked over his shoulder at her and grinned. "I really irritate you on a personal level, don't I? I mean, this is more than me buying up Main Street, isn't it?"

Yes, it really was. Bella stiffened instinctively. The fact that he didn't even *know* why she loathed him was just infuriating. She couldn't tell him what he'd so obviously and embarrassingly forgotten.

"What do you want, Mr. King?"

He frowned a little. "Bella, we've known each other too long to stand on ceremony."

"We don't know each other at all," she corrected. He was going to call her Bella whether she wanted him to or not, it seemed.

"I know you love your shop," Jesse said, moving back to the counter. And her.

Why did he have to smell so good? And did his

eyes really have to be the deep, dark blue of the ocean? Did his smile *have* to cause dimples in his cheeks? And why had the sun bleached out lighter-colored streaks in his dark blond hair? Wasn't he gorgeous enough?

"You've got some nice stuff in here," he said, looking down into the glass display case at the sunglasses, flip-flops and tote bags. "Good eye for color, too. We're a lot alike, you and I. My company makes swimwear. So do you."

She laughed.

He scowled. "What's so funny?"

"Oh, nothing," she said, bracing her hands on the glass countertop. "It's just that my suits are handmade by local women from custom-woven organically sound fabrics and yours are stitched together by children hunched over dirty tables in sweatshops somewhere."

"I don't run sweatshops," he snapped.

"Are you so sure?"

"Yeah, I am. I'm not some Viking here to pillage and burn," he reminded her.

"Might as well be," she muttered. "You've changed the whole face of downtown in less than a year."

"And retail shopping is up 22 percent. I *should* be shot."

She simmered like a pot about to boil over. "There's more to life than profit."

"Yes, there's surfing. And there's great sex." He grinned again, clearly waiting to see if she'd be affected.

Bella would never let him know just how much that smile and his dimples did affect her. Or the casual mention of great sex. Women came too easily to Jesse King. She'd learned that lesson three years ago, when she'd been a card-carrying member of that adoring throng.

The World Surf competition had been in town and Morgan Beach partied for a week. Bella had been on the pier, watching the waves, when Jesse King had strolled up. He'd smiled then, too. And flirted. And teased. He'd kissed her in the moonlight, then taken her to the small bar at the end of the pier where they'd toasted each other with too many margaritas.

She could admit now that she'd been flattered by his attention. He was gorgeous. Famous. And, she'd thought back then, really a very nice guy underneath all the glamour.

That night, they'd wandered together along the sand, until the crowded pier and beach were far behind them. Then they stood at the ocean's edge and watched moonlight dance on the waves.

When Jesse kissed her, Bella was swept away by the magic of the moment and the heat and the delirious sensation of being *wanted.* They'd made love on the sand, with the sea wind rushing over them and the pulsing throb of the ocean whispering in the background.

Bella had seen stars.

Jesse had seen just one of the crowd.

She'd actually gone to see him the following day, in the harsh glare of sunlight. She'd wanted to talk to him about what had happened.

He'd said, "Good to see ya, babe," and walked right past her. He hadn't even remembered having sex with her. She was too stunned to even shout at him. She'd simply stared after him as he walked out of her life.

Bella looked at him now, and remembered every minute of their night together and the humiliation of the day after. But even that hadn't been enough to take away the luscious memory of lying in his arms in the moonlight.

She hated knowing that one night with Jesse had pretty much ruined her for other men. And she *really* hated knowing that he still didn't remember her. But then, why would he?

But not her.

At least, not again.

Everyone made mistakes, but only an idiot made the *same* mistake repeatedly.

Inhaling sharply, Bella told him, "Look, there's no point in arguing anymore. You've already won and I have a business to run. So if you're not here to tell me you're evicting me, I really have to get back to work."

"Evicting you? Why would I do that?"

"You own the building and I've done nothing but try to get rid of you for months."

"Yeah," he said, "but as you pointed out already, I've won that battle. What would be the point of evicting you?"

"Then why are you here?"

"To let you know about the coming rehab."

"Fine," Bella said. "Now I know. Thanks a bunch. Goodbye."

He grinned again and Bella's stomach pitched wildly.

"You know," Jesse said, "when a woman doesn't like me, I've just got to find out why."

"I've already told you why."

"There's more to it than that," he said, his gaze fixed on her. "Trust me when I say I will figure it out."

Two

Jesse couldn't figure out why he was still thinking about Bella. Why the scent of her still clung to him. Why one badly dressed woman with magic eyes was haunting him hours later. Clearly, he told himself, he'd been working too hard.

"According to research, women's beachwear outsells comparable styles for men two to one," Dave said.

Jesse's train of thought cut off as he leaned back in his desk chair. The fact that he actually *had* a desk chair hardly bothered him anymore.

"Dave," Jesse said, as patiently as he could, "I've told you already. I don't have any interest in catering to women—in the stores at least," he added with a smile.

"You're missing out on a gold mine, Mr. King," the

short, balding man said hurriedly. "And if you'll just give me one more moment of your time, I could show you what I mean."

Dave Michaels was the head buyer for King Beach and was constantly trying to push Jesse into expansion. But Jesse had a firm policy. He only sold products he knew and used personally. Products he believed in. Growing up as a King, he'd learned early on that success meant loving what you did. Knowing your business better than anyone else.

But he realized that Dave wouldn't give up until he'd had his chance to make a pitch.

"Fine, let's hear it." Jesse stood up, though, hating the feeling of being trapped behind a desk. Even though his desk was a sleek combination of chrome and glass, it always called up memories of his dad behind a mahogany desk the size of an aircraft carrier, waving at his sons, telling them to go and play, that he was too busy to join them.

Irritated at the memory, he turned his back on Dave to wander the perimeter of his office. Absently, he noticed the shelves filled with the trophies he'd won over the years. On the dark blue walls, there were framed photos of him in competitions, seascapes of some of his favorite beaches and assorted shots of his family. His lucky surfboard was propped up in one corner and the windows behind his desk offered a view of Main Street and the ocean beyond.

As if he needed that connection with the ocean he loved, Jesse moved to the windows and fixed his gaze on the water. Sunlight glinted off the surface of the sea and seemed to spotlight the lucky bastards waiting for the next ride atop their boards. That's where he should be, he thought wryly. How had he come to this, he wondered, not for the first time. How had he ended up exactly in his father's place?

His brothers were probably laughing their asses off just thinking about it.

"There's a store here in town with the kind of products we should be carrying," Dave was saying.

Jesse hardly heard the man. He was willing to do the job that he'd created for himself, but that didn't mean it would ever be his life's blood. Unlike the rest of his family, Jesse considered himself the anti-King, he thought with a half smile. He liked the money, liked the way he lived his life, liked the perks that being successful gave him. So he did the job, but it wasn't who he was. The job was simply that.

Work.

He did what he had to do so that he could do what he wanted to do. Enjoy life. Surf. Date gorgeous women. He wasn't going to end up like his dad—a man who'd devoted everything to the King family dynasty and never really lived.

"If you'll only look at these photos, I'm sure you'll see that her products would be a perfect fit to King Beach's apparel line."

"*Her* products?"

"I know, I know," Dave countered quickly, holding up one hand to forestall Jesse's objections. "You don't want to add women's sportswear to the line, but if you'll just look…"

Jesse laughed shortly. "You just don't give up, do you Dave?"

"Not when I'm right."

"You should have been born a King," Jesse told him and reluctantly took the photos Dave was holding out to him. The sooner he finished work, the sooner he was out there in the sunlight.

"What am I looking at here?" Jesse asked, flipping through the stack of color photos. Bikinis. Sarongs. Beach cover-ups. All pretty, he supposed, but he didn't understand Dave's excitement. Nice enough swimsuits, Jesse thought, though he preferred his bikinis wrapped around gorgeous blondes.

"These suits," Dave said, "are growing in popularity. They're custom-designed, handcrafted with all 'green' fabrics, and the women who buy them swear there's nothing else like them."

Jesse suddenly had a bad feeling.

"There was a write-up in the Sunday magazine section of the newspaper last month and from the reports I'm getting, her sales are going through the roof."

Oh, yeah. That bad feeling kept getting…worse.

Jesse studied the photos more carefully. Some of them looked familiar. As in, he'd seen one of them just yesterday, tacked up to a wall in a crumbling shop on Main Street. "Bella's Beachwear?"

"Yes!" Dave grinned, pointed at one of the photos and said, "That one?" A cherry-red bikini. "My wife bought that one last week. Said it's the most flattering, comfortable suit she's ever owned and she wondered why *we* didn't offer something like it."

"It's nice that your wife's happy with her purchase," Jesse started.

"It's not just my wife, Mr. King," Dave interrupted, his eyes shining with enthusiasm. "Since we moved the business to Morgan Beach, all we've heard about is Bella's. She's got women coming in from all over the state to buy her suits."

Dave kept talking. "One of our guys in accounting did a projection. If we added her line to ours, the sky would literally be the limit on how well she'd do. That's not even saying how her line would influence King Beach sales."

Jesse shook his head. Though he was King enough to appreciate the thought of higher profit margins and headier success, he had his own plan for his business and when he branded women's wear, he would do it his way.

Dave told him flatly, "She's carved out a slice of the consumer pie that no one had really touched on before. We've checked into her and she's had other offers from major sportswear companies to buy her out, but she's turned them all down."

Intrigued in spite of himself, Jesse leaned back against the edge of his desk, folded his arms over his chest and said simply, "Explain."

Warming to his theme, Dave did. "Most swimsuits in this country and, hell, everywhere else, are designed and created for the so-called 'ideal' woman. A skinny one."

Jesse smiled. Skinny women in bikinis. What's not to smile about? Although he usually preferred a little more meat on his women.

As if he could read Jesse's mind, Dave said, "The majority of American women don't meet that standard. And thank God for it. Most women are curvy. They eat more than a lettuce leaf. And thanks to most designers, their needs are overlooked."

"You know, Dave, I like curves on a woman as much as the next guy," Jesse told him, "but not all women should wear a bikini. If Bella wants to sell to women who probably shouldn't be wearing suits anyway, let her do it. It's not for us."

Dave grimaced, then reached into his pocket for another photo. "I thought that would be your reaction," he said tightly. "So I came prepared. Look at this."

Jesse took the photo and his eyebrows lifted. "This is your wife."

"Yeah," Dave said, grinning now. "Normally Connie bans all cameras when we go swimming. Since she bought this suit, I couldn't get her to stop posing."

Jesse could understand why. Connie Michaels had given birth to three children over the last six years. She wasn't skinny, but she wasn't fat, either. And in the swimsuit she had purchased from Bella, she looked…great.

"She's really beautiful," Jesse mused.

Instantly, Dave plucked the photo from his hand. "Yeah, I think so. But my point is, if Bella's suits look this good on a normal-size woman, they'd look great on the skinny ones, too. I'm telling you, Mr. King, this is something you should think about."

"Fine. I'll think about it," Jesse told him, more to get Dave to drop the subject than anything else.

"Her sales are building steadily and I think she'd be a great asset to King Beach."

"Asset." Jesse murmured the word, remembering the look on Bella's face that morning during their "conversation." Oh, yeah. She'd already turned down offers from other companies. He could just see how pleased she'd be with *his* offer to buy out her business. Hell, she'd probably run him down with her car.

Not that it was going to be an issue because, "We don't sell women's wear yet."

Dave took a breath and said, "Word is Pipeline is looking to court Bella's Beachwear."

"Pipeline?" Jesse's major competitor, Nick Acona, ran Pipeline clothing and the fact that neither of them surfed anymore didn't get rid of the rivalry. If Nick was interested in Bella—that was almost enough to get Jesse involved.

"He says the way to increased sales is through women," Dave told him.

Jesse gave his assistant a hard look. He knew exactly what Dave was up to. And it was working. "I'll consider it."

"But—"

"Dave," he asked, "do you like your job?"

Dave grinned. He'd heard that threat before and didn't put much stock in it. "Yes, sir."

"Good. Let's keep it that way."

"Right." The man gathered up his notes, his research and the photos and headed for the door. "You did say you'd think about it, though."

"And I will." The truth was he knew he should expand into women's beachwear. He just hadn't found any he'd believed in enough to stock. Until now. The challenge would be in convincing Bella to come on board—before Pipeline got their hooks in her.

When Dave was gone, a spot of color caught his eye and Jesse bent down to pick up off the floor a photo Dave had left behind. A sea-green bikini with narrow straps on the halter top and silver rings at the hips, holding the bottom together.

Jesse caught himself trying to imagine Bella wearing that suit. He couldn't quite bring it off, though, and that was irritating, too. She wore those big, blousy tops and shapeless skirts, deliberately hiding her figure. Was it a studied plan to drive a man nuts?

Smiling to himself, Jesse tossed the photo onto his desk, turned around and looked down Main Street to Bella's place. He couldn't seem to get her out of his head. He kept remembering the battle-ready glint in her eye. Even if she dressed like a disaster refugee, there was something about her that…

Nope, forget it. He wasn't interested in Bella Cruz.

But there *was* a certain woman in Morgan Beach he was looking for. His mystery woman.

Narrowing his gaze on the sea, Jesse thought back to one night three years ago. He didn't remember much about that night or her… He'd won a huge competition that day and he'd been doing a lot of celebrating before he ran into her. Then there was more celebrating and finally, there was sex on the beach. Amazing, completely staggering, sex.

She'd been at the edges of his mind ever since. He couldn't recall her face, but he knew the sizzle of her touch. He couldn't remember the sound of her voice, but he knew the taste of her.

Oh, it was more than the waves that had brought him to Morgan Beach. His mystery woman was here. Somewhere. At least, he hoped so. She could have been in town for the competition, he supposed, but he liked to think that she lived here. That sooner or later, he'd run across her again.

And this time, when he got his hands on her, he wouldn't let her go.

His phone rang, thankfully silencing his thoughts. Automatically, he turned to snatch it up. "King."

"Jesse, it's Tom Harold. Just checking with you on the photo shoot scheduled for tomorrow."

"Right." More photos. But this was for a national campaign advertising King Beach and its end-of-summer sale. He might not have wanted to become a businessman, but now that he was, the King blood in his veins refused to let him be anything but a success.

"Yeah, we're set, Tom." He turned back to the window and stared out at the ocean. "The models will arrive first thing in the morning, and you can do the shoot on the beach. The mayor's cleared it for us to rope a section off."

"Perfect. I'll be there."

Jesse hung up, sat down at his desk and shoved thoughts of Bella out of his mind. There was plenty of paperwork—the one sure way to keep his thoughts too busy to wander.

"For Pete's sake, Bella," Kevin Walters told her over dinner that night, "stop antagonizing the man. Do you *want* him to end your lease?"

Kevin, with his dark red hair, tanned skin and blue eyes was Bella's best friend. They'd known each other for five years, ever since Bella had moved to Morgan Beach and rented her house from him. She could talk to him as she would any girlfriend and he was usually willing to give her the guy's point of view when she needed it. Tonight, however, she'd really rather he saw things from *her* perspective.

"No, I don't," she said quickly. She still had two months left on her lease and if Jesse King tossed her out, she'd have to sell suits out of her rental house; she didn't think Kevin would be thrilled with that solution. Which was just one more reason to be mad at Jesse King.

"You know, another couple of years in my location and I could have bought my house from you—"

He held up one hand. "I've offered to make you a deal."

"I don't need special deals, Kevin. You know I want to do this myself."

"Yeah, I know."

Reaching across the table to give his hand a pat,

Bella said, "I really do appreciate that you want to help me buy the place, Kevin. It's just that it wouldn't really be mine if I didn't do it all myself."

"Right. Like that shirt you're wearing?" He pointed to the heavily appliquéd, long-sleeved yellow muslin shirt that she wore with her best black skirt. "That's yours, right? So what? You did the weaving yourself? Stitched it all together and did the little flowers around the collar?"

"No…"

"So houses and shirts are different?"

"Well, yeah."

He shook his head and sighed. "Fine. Good. You want to buy the house and if you make King mad enough, he'll end your lease and then no house. So why continue to piss him off?"

Bella used her fork to poke at her vegetarian lasagna, then gave it up and dropped the fork to her plate with a clatter. Folding her arms atop the table, she looked at Kevin. "Because he doesn't even *remember* me. It's infuriating. Humiliating."

She'd confessed all one night during a monster movie marathon. And Kevin had immediately told her that she should have reminded Jesse of who she was when she'd run into him the following day. Of course he had. He was a guy.

Kevin shrugged and took a bite of his zucchini and potato casserole. "So tell him."

"*Tell* him?" Bella just stared at him. "You know, maybe I'd have been better off with a girl for a best friend. I wouldn't have to explain to another woman why *telling* Jesse that we'd slept together was a bad idea. She would know that instinctively."

Grinning, Kevin said, "Yes, but a girl best friend wouldn't come next door at ten at night to unclog your shower drain."

"Good point," Bella said. "But you've got a blind spot when it comes to Jesse."

"God, women always make everything harder than it has to be," Kevin muttered with a shake of his head. "This is why the battle of the sexes exists, you know. Because you guys are always on the battlefield ready for war and we're standing around on the sidelines saying, 'What's she mad about?'"

Bella laughed at the irritation in his gaze, which didn't appease him much.

"Let me guess," Kevin said with a tired sigh. "This is one of those If-he-doesn't-know-why-I'm-mad-I'm-sure-not-going-to-tell-him things, isn't it?"

"Yeah. And it's not a 'thing', it just is. He should know," Bella snapped and reached for her wineglass. "For Pete's sake, are there so many women in his wake that we're all just blurs to him?"

"Bella, honey," Kevin said, leaning back in the red leather booth, "you know I love you. But that is so female it has nothing to do with the world of man."

He was right and she knew it. Men and women came at the whole *sex* thing from completely different mind-sets. Even though she'd had too many margaritas that night, Bella had made a conscious decision to sleep with Jesse. And it hadn't been because he was rich or famous or gorgeous.

But because they'd really *talked* to each other. She'd felt a connection to him that she'd never felt before to anyone. That was the only reason she'd done what she did. Jesse, though, she realized by the next day, had only had sex with her because she was there. Willing. There'd been no meaning in it for him at all.

"If you wanted more from him than one night, you should have said something the next day," Kevin told her. "Made him remember. But no. Instead, you went all female on him and left him in the dark."

"I didn't put him in the dark," Bella reminded him.

For at least the tenth time, Bella went back over her conversation with Jesse King that morning three years ago. He'd looked right at her. Given her all his most practiced moves and never once remembered that they'd had sex! The man had had so many women, she'd been lost in the crowd from the moment she gave herself to him.

"Look, I know you don't like the guy, but he's here now and he's not going away," Kevin pointed out around another bite of his dinner. "He's moved the corporate offices here, he's opened his flagship store in town. Jesse King is here to stay, like it or not, and no protest is going to change that."

"I know," she grumbled.

"So if you're going to live in the same town with him, tell him what's bugging you. Otherwise, you're gonna drive yourself insane."

"You know," Bella told him, "I wasn't really looking for logic, here. I just wanted to enjoy my rant."

"Ah. Okay then, rant away. I'm listening."

"Sure, but you're not agreeing," she said, smiling.

"Nope, I'm not." Kevin shrugged. "I'm sorry you hate him and everything, but he seems like a nice enough guy to me."

"That's only because he bought that gold-and-emerald necklace from you." Kevin's store stocked work by local artists and jewelry designers, so he was always happy when he made a big sale.

He smiled and sighed. "Yeah, gotta say, a guy who spends a few thousand on a custom-made necklace without batting an eye? My kind of customer."

"Fine, fine. You're happy. The town's happy. Jesse's happy." She shoved her lasagna around on the plate. "I wrote a lctter to the editor of the local paper."

"Uh-oh," Kevin muttered. "What kind of letter?"

She winced, regretting now what she'd done, but it was way too late to call it back. "Something about the corporations of America ruining small-town life."

He laughed. "Bella…"

"They probably won't even run it."

"Of course they will," he said. "Then you can expect another visit from Jesse King." Kevin paused, tipped his head to one side and looked at her. "Or is that what this is all about? You actually *want* him coming around, don't you?"

"No, I don't," she argued, wishing Kevin were just a little less observant. Could *she* help it if every time

Jesse King walked through her door she felt a zing of something amazing? It wasn't her fault that her hormones reacted when he was in the room. Heck, every female in America suffered from the same symptoms when it came to Jesse King.

And the very fact that he affected her so much was exactly *why* she was so bent on making him miserable. She probably should stop antagonizing him, as Kevin said, but she just couldn't bring herself to.

Bella had fought Jesse's takeover of Morgan Beach with everything she had. And still, she'd lost. He'd moved in, bought up property and immediately started ruining the only place she'd ever called home.

An only child, Bella had lost her parents at seven, gone into a series of nice, if impersonal foster homes and when she turned eighteen, she was out on her own. She didn't mind it so much, though the pangs for family never quite left her.

She'd put herself through college by making clothes for the girls who didn't have to worry about saving every cent. She'd sewn and knitted and crocheted her way to an education. Then she'd taken her first vacation ever, stumbled across Morgan Beach and never left.

She'd been here five years and she loved it. The tiny coastal town was everything she'd always dreamed of in a hometown. Small, friendly and close enough to big retail she could always indulge in a fun shopping trip when she felt the need. Even better, the close-knit feeling of the community fed that lack of family she'd always felt. People here cared about each other.

Now, with Jesse here, her beloved small town felt almost claustrophobic.

"Sell it to somebody else, Bella," Kevin said laughing. "Every time you say the guy's name, your eyes go all soft and shiny."

"They do not." Did they? Well, that was embarrassing as all get-out.

"Oh, yeah, they do, and I'll prove it. Look out the window."

She turned her head to glance out the window onto Main Street and was just in time to see Jesse King walking by. His dark blond, sun-streaked hair was too long. His blue jeans were faded and molded to his long legs and the white long-sleeved shirt he wore only accentuated his tan.

She sighed.

"Gotcha," Kevin said.

"You're so evil," Bella told him, but couldn't tear her gaze away from the man who was still occupying far too much of her thoughts.

Three

By the next morning, Bella had convinced herself that Kevin was right. She'd just have to suck it up and talk to Jesse. Tell him just what she thought of a man who could make love to a woman one night and forget her existence the following morning. She'd get everything off her chest and then she'd be fine.

She'd be over him.

Bella paused in front of her shop for a moment, and smiled to herself. Even Jesse King couldn't quash the thrill she experienced every time she walked into the world she'd built with her own talent.

But even as she enjoyed the sight of her place, once Jesse's "rehab" was finished, it would lose all its character. The creak in the front door would be "fixed." The pockmarked walls would be smoothed. The floor would be carpeted, all the gleaming floorboards covered up. Bella's Beachwear would survive, but it wouldn't be the same. The man had no more vision when it came to business than he had when it came to women.

It was all about the bottom line to men like Jesse.

A crowd was gathering across the street on the beach and she turned her head to look. As a few dozen people milled around, Bella caught glimpses of what was going on. She noticed the RVs parked on the sand, a bank of cameras, huge lights and electric fans. And in the middle of it all, Jesse King.

In spite of herself, she was curious. Bella hurried across Pacific Coast Highway and stepped up onto the sidewalk. She kept to the fringes of the interested crowd of onlookers and let her gaze slide over the goings-on.

Gorgeous male models, each of them wearing King Beachwear, were positioned around several surfboards, all planted nose down in the sand. Bella had to admit that the guys looked great, but her gaze kept straying to the female models they were using in the background. "Honestly, you'd think he could take a *little* interest in what the women were wearing."

"Why am I not surprised you've got a comment?"

She whipped her head around and looked up into Jesse's amused blue eyes. He'd managed to sneak up on her. Darn it.

"Let's hear it," he said, one corner of his mouth tipping up as he folded his arms across his chest. He glanced at the photo shoot, saw the photographer bustling around, arranging everything to his satisfaction. "What don't you like about all this?"

Bella bit down on her bottom lip. It wasn't any of her business, of course and she really shouldn't care at all, but then…her gaze went back to the very pretty, very thin women wearing generic swimsuits and she just couldn't stand it. "If you're going to all this trouble to shoot a big ad campaign, why not have *all* of the models look good?"

He frowned at her. "They do."

"Why do I bother?" she muttered, shaking her head. "Look at the blond girl in the back."

He did and smiled at the view.

Bella ignored that. "Her suit doesn't fit right. It's too tight across her hips—what there are of them—and too big at the bust."

"She looks fine to me," Jesse said with a shrug.

Bella pushed a strand of windblown hair out of her eyes, then pointed at a brunette talking to one of the male models. "What about her? That bikini is cut all wrong and the fabric is shiny, for heaven's sake. What did you do? Go down to the department store and snatch a bunch of suits off the clearance rack?"

Jesse frowned. "The girls look okay to me. Besides, this shoot isn't about *women's* suits. It's about King Beach. We're selling *guys'* clothes. The girls are just background."

"Do they have to be poorly fitted background?" she asked.

He sighed a little. "We've got a contract. We're giving the department store—"

"Hah!" she crowed, because she'd been so right about where they'd purchased the women's suits.

He scowled at her. "The store gets credit in the photo tagline."

"Fine," she said, wondering why she even cared about any of this. "Use one or two of them. But if you want this ad to look good, then *all* the models should be eye-catching."

One eyebrow lifted. "Meaning…"

She shouldn't have walked over here, she told herself. Shouldn't have gotten involved. What did it matter to her, after all, if his magazine ad didn't look as good as it could? Yet…

Bella's gaze slid back to the swimsuits the women were wearing and every one of her designer instincts stood up and growled. She simply couldn't stand it. Besides, Jesse King was so darn sure of himself. So arrogant, she really wanted to… "Meaning, women are the real shoppers of the world, Mr. King. If you had any sense, you'd know that. Those suits your models are wearing are so generic they should be marked *one size fits all* as long as they're size 0s. My suits are made to flatter a woman's figure. All women."

He grinned, looked her up and down, then stared into her eyes with a direct challenge. "Even you?"

Insulted, Bella lifted her chin and glared at him. She knew she was being manipulated, but at the moment, Bella didn't even care. He was so convinced that his way was the right way, she wanted to prove him completely wrong. One sure way to do that was to show him exactly what she meant.

"I'll be right back," she announced, then left him to walk over to the female models. She spoke to them briefly, got their sizes, then hurried across the street to her shop. It only took a few minutes for Bella to scurry back to the photo shoot, her arms filled with some of her designer suits.

"What do you think you're doing?" Jesse asked as she herded the women toward one of the RV trailers.

"You're about to find out," was all she said as she stepped into the trailer behind the models and firmly closed the door.

Minutes ticked past and Jesse frowned at the RV. He wasn't sure why he was letting Bella get away with this. He should have just headed her off at the pass, so to speak, and told her he didn't need her help to sell *his* sportswear. But damn if he'd been able to do that.

"Jesse, how much longer?"

He turned to look at Tom, the photographer, then shot a quick glance at his own wristwatch. "Give her another few minutes, Tom. As soon as she admits she was wrong to stick her nose in, we'll get back to the shoot."

"Fine by me," Tom told him, shifting a fast look at the cobalt-blue sky above. "But we've only got this section of the beach for the morning."

"You're right." Jesse's permit would end at noon, so there was no point in indulging Bella any further, even to get her to admit that she was wrong. He stalked over to the RV and knocked on the door. "Bella," he called out, "time's up. We need to finish the shoot."

The door to the RV opened and the models came out, smiling and primping. Jesse checked out each and every one of them as they walked past him. Even the skinniest of the models looked as if she had a figure now. The fabrics clung to their bodies and enhanced what few curves they had. It cost him to think it, but Bella had been right.

Tom, the photographer, let loose a low whistle and instantly started staging the women into far more prominent poses for the ad shoot. Jesse watched and shook his head, amazed, really, at the transformation. But where the hell was Bella?

Smiling to himself, he climbed the steps into the RV, stuck his head inside and shouted, "Lose your nerve? C'mon Bella, let's see you in one of those suits you're so proud of."

"Turn around." The sound of her voice came from right behind him and Jesse couldn't figure out how she'd gotten past him. But when he turned to look at her, he understood completely.

For months, he'd seen the woman around town, always buried under mountains of fabric. He'd naturally assumed that she had a body she was trying to hide.

He couldn't have been more wrong.

"Bella?" His gaze moved over her in a quick, thorough glance, then he looked again, giving her a more leisurely going over. The woman had enough curves to make any man sit up and beg.

"Wow," he said, walking a slow, tight circle around her, "you look..." *Familiar* was what he wanted to say, but he couldn't figure out why that would be, so he let it go in favor of, "amazing."

The bikini she wore was a deep red and clung to her body like a lover's hands. Her breasts were high and full, her waist was small, her hips rounded and just above her behind, at the small of her back, a tiny tattoo of the sun peeked at him. Her skin was smooth and the color of warm honey. Her long, dark brown hair hung down her back and swayed with her every movement. And her chocolate eyes were watching him with satisfaction.

"Thanks," she said, fisting her hands at her bare hips. "I believe I've made my point."

He grinned at her. "What point was that?"

"That the right bathing suit makes all the difference."

"Honey," he said, "with a body like that, you could wear one of *my* suits and look amazing."

She shook her head and he was fascinated with the way her hair danced and swayed. His body felt tight and need was a clamoring beast inside him. It was all he could do to keep his hands to himself, when what he *wanted* to do was pull her in close, kiss her until she couldn't talk and then find the closest flat surface, lay her down on it and bury himself inside her.

But judging from the fire flashing in her eyes at the moment, that little fantasy wasn't going to come true anytime soon.

"You're incredible," she said softly.

"What's that supposed to mean?"

"I only dressed your models—and myself—to prove

to you that I was right. That your way of doing things, mass-produced swimwear, isn't the *only* way. That *my* way is better."

"Not the way to make your fortune, though," he said, leaning one shoulder against the doorjamb as she gathered up her tentlike blouse and skirt.

"Who says I'm interested in that?" she demanded, whipping her hair out of her eyes long enough to glare at him.

"You're a businesswoman. Why wouldn't you want to succeed?"

"Success doesn't *have* to be your way."

"My way's not bad." It occurred to him that he was defending his business. The very business he had never intended to start. "Contracting out to manufacturers streamlines the business, allows you to reach more customers and—"

"—And cuts you off from the customers, too," she added. "You get so big you forget why you started your business in the first place. But that doesn't matter to a King, does it?" She walked close, poked him in the chest with her index finger and said, "Your whole family—you're like warlords or something. You swoop in, buy up what you want and never consider any way but yours."

"Hey, now," he argued, grabbing her finger and closing his fist around it. Warmth shot through him with the first contact of her skin against his, shattering his thoughts, obliterating whatever it was he'd been about to say.

He remembered feeling like this once before with the touch of a woman's skin. Remembered the slide of her skin against his, the heat of their joining, the taste of her mouth, the tight fit of his body locked inside hers. And just for a second, Jesse stared at her, refusing to believe that Bella Cruz might be his mystery woman.

"What are you doing?" she asked, trying to tug her hand free of his grasp. "Why are you looking at me like that?"

"No way," he murmured, more to himself than to her. It couldn't be. Not her. Not the woman who had been a thorn in his side from day one.

"What?" This time she succeeded in pulling free of him and then she took a hasty step or two backward just for good measure. "Look, um, I've got to get to my shop. I've spent too much time here already and—"

"Just a minute," he said, moving toward her, letting the RV door swing closed behind him. Inside, the trailer was filled with shadows, sunlight drifting through louvered shades on the windows. The scent of coffee and perfume hung in the air and from outside came the shouts and laughter of the crowd gathered to watch the photo shoot.

Jesse paid no attention to any of it. All he could see was her. Her chocolate eyes watched him warily even as he told himself that the only sure way to know if Bella was actually his mystery woman was to kiss her. To taste her. And damn if she was leaving this trailer until he'd done just that.

"Mr. King," she said, looking around as if for an exit

that wasn't barred by his tall, broad body, "*Jesse,* I really do need to get going now."

"Yeah," he said, moving closer still until her breath fanned against his chin as she looked up at him. "I know. But there's just one more thing we have to do first."

She licked her lips. "What's that?"

He smiled and dipped his head. "This," he whispered, then took her mouth with his.

She went stiff as a board for about a split second, then pliant, leaning into him, wrapping her arms around his neck. He pulled her in close, his hands at her waist, his fingertips nearly burning with the heat her skin engendered. Her lips parted under his and his tongue swept into her warmth and he knew.

That taste of her was something he would never forget. Something he'd been dreaming about for three years. He finally had her in his arms again. Finally could hold her, taste her, touch her and as realization flooded him, he broke the kiss abruptly, stared down into her glazed, dark brown eyes and said, "It's *you.*"

She staggered a little. "What?"

"You. On the beach. Three years ago."

She blinked up at him, rubbed her fingertips across her mouth and then drew in a long, shaky breath. "Congratulations," she said at last. "You finally remembered."

"You knew?" he demanded. "You remembered and didn't say anything to me?"

"Why would I?" she asked, gathering up the clothes

she'd dropped when he was kissing her. "You think I'm *proud* of that night?"

"You ought to be," he told her sharply. "We were great together."

"We were strangers. It was a huge mistake."

She tried to get past him, but Jesse grabbed her upper arm and stopped her dead. "I looked for you. The next day, I went back to the beach and looked all over."

"You thought I'd just be lying there on the sand, waiting for you?"

"That's not what I meant, damn it. But where the hell were you?"

Bella pushed her hand through her hair and glared at him. "You didn't look for me very hard. I went to see you the next morning and you blew right past me."

Frowning, Jesse tried to remember that, but truthfully, he'd been celebrating so much that most of that night and the following morning was a blur. All he'd really known was the touch of her. The taste of her. "When you saw me, did you tell me who you were?"

"Of course not!" This time, she did push past him, dragging her arm from his grasp.

"Well, how the hell would I know who you were otherwise?" he asked.

"Oh!" She looked at him the way she would a splotch of mud on her shirt. "What kind of man can't remember what the woman he's had sex with looks like?"

"One with a hangover," he told her. "As I recall, we both had a few margaritas that night."

"Yes, but I still knew who you were," she snapped, then

took a long, deep breath and said, "You said you went looking for me. Just how did you plan to identify me?"

"I don't know…" He scrubbed one hand across his jaw and over the back of his neck. "Dammit, Bella, you could have told me—if not the morning after, then any time since I came to town." He tilted his head to one side and studied her. "Is this why you've been so mad at me?"

"Please," she said with a sniff and a lift of her chin. "Could you think any more highly of yourself? This isn't personal, Jesse," she told him as she grabbed the doorknob and twisted it. "This is about you taking over my town. Don't you get it? I hate you and everything you stand for."

"You can't hate me," he told her, bracing one hand on the wall and leaning in toward her. "You don't know me well enough to hate me."

She laughed shortly, but her eyes didn't shine with humor. "I got to 'know' you well enough three years ago."

"Yeah," he said softly, "well, I think it's time we got to know each other all over again."

"Never. Going. To. Happen," she told him and opened the door.

"Never say never, Bella," he called after her and when she slammed the door, Jesse grinned. Three years he'd been thinking about that woman. And he wasn't going to rest until he got her back where he wanted her. In his bed.

Nothing a King liked better than a challenge.

"Get Dave Michaels in here," Jesse told his assistant as he stalked toward his office.

He closed the door, walked directly to the window

overlooking Main Street, Bella's shop and the ocean. He told himself he wanted to stare at the sea for a few minutes, gather his thoughts, let the never-ending roll and slap of the waves ease his mind as it always did.

But the truth was, he was watching Bella's shop.

"Dammit, why'd it have to be her?" he whispered, shoving both hands into the pockets of his slacks. His mystery woman had dogged his thoughts off and on for three years. After that one amazing night on the beach with her, he'd hung around town for a couple of weeks searching for her in every face he met. But she'd seemed to have disappeared. Hell, he'd actually come here to settle in Morgan Beach on the off chance that he might find her again.

"Karma really is a bitch," he muttered.

Sunlight spilled through the window and if the glass hadn't been tinted, Jesse would have been half-blinded by the brilliance of the light. The air conditioner clicked on and a soft hum of cool air pumped into the room. Even at the beach, September temperatures could spike into some serious heat.

There was a knock on his door, then Dave walked in asking, "You wanted to see me?"

Jesse turned and nodded. "Tell me everything you know about Bella Cruz."

Dave's face lit up. "Seriously? You're considering expanding?"

Was he? Yes, he was. He might not have started out wanting to be a businessman. But he'd become one anyway. And as a King, he wasn't going to do the job half-assed. That meant that it was time to stop treating King Beach like a hobby. He was going to make his company the biggest name in surf gear and swimwear in the world. To do that, he needed to get female customers.

Bella was his ticket there.

She might not know it yet, but it was only a matter of time before both Bella herself *and* her swimsuit line were taken over by Jesse King.

"Where do you want me to start?" Dave asked, walking into the office and dropping into one of the chairs opposite Jesse's desk.

"Personal," Jesse said flatly. "Family. Boyfriends. Husbands and/or exes. I want it all."

Dave frowned. "I thought this was about her business."

"It is," Jesse assured him, sitting down behind his desk. He leaned an elbow on the arm of his chair, watched the man opposite him and said, "To get the jump on Pipeline, I've got to move fast. That means having as much information as possible."

"It just seems sneaky."

"It's good business," Jesse told him. "Besides, to defeat your opponent, you have to know her first."

"Opponent?" Dave echoed, sounding a little uneasy. "She's not an opponent."

Jesse sighed, then grinned. "How long have you and Connie been married, Dave?"

"Thirteen years, why?"

"You've been out of the dating game so long, you've forgotten what it's really like." Jesse sat forward to lay his forearms on the desktop and continued, "Women and men are *always* opposing forces. That's the fun, after all. If we understood women, where would the challenge be?"

"Why does it have to be a challenge?"

Jesse chuckled. "Doesn't have to be," he said. "It just is. The trick is, knowing the woman you're interested in, figuring out how her mind works, if you can. Once you do that, everything comes more easily."

"If you say so," Dave said, but he didn't sound as if he believed him.

"Trust me on this. If I want to win Bella over, keep her from signing with Pipeline, then I've got to know her, don't I?"

"I guess you do," Dave said, then smiled. "I think Bella's stuff is going to be great for King Beach."

Jesse nodded. "It will. I'll see to it. But until I convince Bella of that, our plans are top secret. Nobody knows. Not even Connie."

Dave winced, then shrugged. "You got it, boss."

"Good." Jesse listened as Dave started talking, giving him all the information he had on Bella.

And while Dave talked, Jesse began to plan the way he would prove to Bella just how much *she* needed *him.*

Four

For the next couple of days, Jesse watched a steady stream of customers go in and out of Bella's shop. From the vantage point of his office window or from a seat in the sidewalk café on the beach, he had a perfect view of Bella's Beachwear and its all-too-intriguing owner. What had astounded Jesse was the *amount* of business she did. Bella had told him that her business was slowing down because the season was over. Well, if this was slow, he was impressed.

He still didn't like the idea of expanding. But he couldn't get the facts out of his head, either. Dave's research proved just how successful Bella had become in her niche market, and damn if he'd let Nick Acona grab up her business right from under his nose.

She was the perfect advertisement for her wares. A normal-size woman walked into her store frustrated by the offerings at chain stores, and left with a smile on her face. He'd been watching it for days.

"And there go two more," he said to no one as he set his hands on either side of his office's wide window and stared down at Main Street. A couple of women were just leaving Bella's, carrying huge, purple-and-white-striped shopping bags that looked stuffed to bursting. She had a good business, he admitted silently, but he could make it great.

If he bought her out, or better yet, simply absorbed her company into his, keeping her on as head designer, they could both make millions. Even though she'd probably fight him every inch of the way. He smiled to himself at the thought. Damn if he didn't like that about her. The way her brown eyes snapped with fury or irritation. The way she lifted her chin and gave him a glare that she fully expected would turn him to stone.

Most women he knew were so busy flirting with him, they'd never consider arguing with him. Bella was different. And now that he knew *she* was his mystcry girl, she was even more appealing.

He wanted her. Badly. The woman he'd been thinking about for three years was here. Right in front of him. Ready to be taken again. He was more than ready to do the taking.

But *taking* wasn't right, either. He wanted to explore that fabulous body, feel the buzz of her skin beneath his and build new memories. Jesse smiled to himself. He wanted more than just one more night with her. He wasn't thinking about how *much* more, but that wasn't the point.

She was.

Hell, Jesse actually liked her. And dammit, he understood her. Watching Bella with her customers, he knew that her business was more than just work to her. He'd felt the same way back when he started. When he bought his first company, he'd actually gone in and learned how to shape and make the surfboards himself. He'd enjoyed being in on the ground floor, feeling a connection to the business that he never would have had simply as a suit. It had made it more than a company to him. It had made it a part of him.

And there was no doubt in his mind that was how Bella felt about her shop. He admired that about her, even as he knew that would be the sticking point to winning her over. She wouldn't want to let go of the reins of her shop.

She was going to be a hard sell. The difference was, he knew her secret. He knew that she was a woman of passion. A woman who'd rocked his world three years ago.

So what he had to do here was seduce her. Charm her. Flatter her. Get her into his bed and once he had her there, he'd be in a position to smooth her into his company.

When it was all over, she'd be rich and thanking him.

If there was one thing Jesse King knew, it was women.

"Jesse King's been with so many women, he can't tell us apart anymore. The entire female gender is like nothing more than a well-stocked candy store. He likes candy, so he just grazes his way through the aisles." Bella scowled and tapped her fingernails against one of the glass jewelry cases in Kevin's shop.

It had been three days since she'd seen Jesse. Three days and he hadn't made an effort to talk to her. Not a phone call. Not one of his annoying drop-ins at her store. Not even a brief sighting on the street. Not that she had been hoping for any of that, but she couldn't help feeling frustrated.

He'd seemed…excited to find out that she was the woman he'd been with three years ago on the beach. So much so that he'd been avoiding her ever since. Bella groaned internally. For heaven's sake, she was angry when he was around and even angrier when he wasn't. "Clearly, he's making me insane."

"Nothing wrong with a little insanity," Kevin told her.

"Easy enough to say when you're not the babbling idiot," Bella muttered and leaned over a glass display case to examine a new pair of earrings Kevin had stocked. "Is this turquoise?"

"God, you're plebian," he said with a laugh. "No, my little peasant, that's lapis lazuli. Antique. That stone—well, not that one in particular—was really popular back in the day with emperors and pharaohs."

"You know," Bella told him, tipping her head to one side and smiling up at him, "if I hadn't met your girlfriend, I'd swear you were gay."

"Straight men know good jewelry, too. Your surfer guy bought that great emerald piece from me, remember?"

Bella felt a twinge. Who had he bought it for? One of his celebrity dates? She had to be important to him. You didn't just buy emeralds for a casual fling. Of course, maybe Jesse did.

"Ah, yes, Mr. Thoughtful. Wonder which one of the slavering crowd gets the emeralds," Bella mused, stopping in front of a display case of sterling silver.

"Honey, you sound like a jealous wife."

Her head snapped up and she pinned him with a hard look. "I do not."

Kevin shrugged. "Yeah, you do."

Oh God, did she really? That was lowering. She wasn't jealous of Jesse's women. She was…heck, she didn't even know *what* she was anymore. Still… "I'm not jealous. I'm irritated."

"And hiding it nicely." Kevin bent over the glass case and looked into her eyes. "So he knows about three years ago."

"Yes, and had the nerve to tell me I should have told him who I was sooner."

"What an idiot," Kevin said chuckling. "Using logic."

"Oh, that's very funny," Bella said. "This has nothing to do with logic, anyway. He was completely insulting."

"Insulting?" Kevin shoved his hands into the pockets of his jeans and rocked back on his heels. "Jeez, Bella. Cut the guy a break."

Bella scowled. "He doesn't need a break from me. He makes his own breaks."

"He told you he remembered that night. Remembered *you.* How is that insulting?" Kevin demanded before adding, "And speak slowly, because I'm working with a Y chromosome here."

"It's insulting because he remembered the sex. He didn't remember *me.*" Then there was the fact that he hadn't bothered to even talk to her once since his memory had been jogged. Oh, yes, being "remembered" by Jesse King was so-o-o flattering.

"Sure he did." Kevin gave a long-suffering sigh. "Women make this so much harder than it has to be. The guy remembered the sex *because* of you. So therefore he remembered you."

"Is it a genetic imperative that guys have to stick together?"

"Against women, hell, yes," Kevin admitted. "I love women, don't get me wrong, but you guys are enough to make a man old before his time."

"I don't know why," Bella said with a sniff. "We make perfect sense to each other."

"Exactly."

"Kevin, could you just be my best friend for a minute and not Jesse's brother-in-arms? Don't you get it? I could have been anyone as far as he knew," Bella argued.

"I *am* your best friend, and that's why I'm telling you the truth even though you don't want to hear it. You weren't just anyone to him. You're you. And he remembered. So cut him some slack."

"I can't believe you're still on his side," Bella said, eyes wide.

"The question is, why are you so against him?" Kevin leaned on the display case and grinned at her. "Seems to me you're awfully obsessed with Jesse."

"I'm not obsessed, I'm…focused," she finished lamely.

"Uh-huh."

Bella scowled at him. "We used to be together on this. Aren't you the one who helped me organize the protest march against corporate takeovers in Morgan Beach?"

He grinned. "You're the only one who's got a problem with him anymore."

"Fine. Lone wolf," she muttered. "That's me."

The bell over the door jangled and he gave her a quick grin. "Be back in a sec, Ms. Wolf, I've got a customer. Take a look at the new sterling earrings. Mrs. Latimer," he called out, hustling over to the tall, richly dressed woman entering the shop. "I've got some new jade you're going to love."

"Things are pretty darn sad when even your best friend isn't on your side," Bella muttered, strolling down the length of the counter again. Her gaze flicked past the gemstones, the twisted gold and the heavier sterling silver.

Kevin's shop sold jewelry made by local artisans. Here you could find everything from exquisite, high-priced jewels to skull rings and pentagrams. Eclectic, she thought. Like the town used to be. She ran her finger over the cool glass. "Jade. Emeralds. Diamonds."

"Which do you prefer?"

Bella felt her jaw drop. "What are you doing here?"

Jesse grinned at her, and carefully closed her mouth with the tip of one finger under her chin. "Came back to see if Kevin got in the matching earrings to a necklace I picked up here a couple of weeks ago."

"Ah, yes, the emeralds." Did she sound wistful? She didn't want to sound wistful.

"You have something against them?"

"Not a thing," Bella said, forcing a smile. "I just hope the woman you're buying them for appreciates the gesture. Hmm," she added, tipping her head to one side as she looked up at him, "I wonder. Do you remember *her* name?"

His eyes flashed and a muscle in his jaw ticked, but that was the only sign her barb had hit home.

"I do," he said. "But now I'm wondering why you care. Jealous?"

"Please." She glanced across the room at Kevin, who wasn't paying the slightest bit of attention to them, focused as he was on his customer. Great. No reprieves headed her way.

She wasn't jealous. She was pissy. Bella stared up into Jesse's beautiful eyes and told herself to remember that she was nothing to him. A blurry memory of one night that he hadn't even been able to recall the morning after.

Okay, that thought helped her weakened knees to strengthen a bit. He was charm personified. He knew just how to break down a woman's defenses. And Bella, despite knowing all that, was just as susceptible as the next woman. Dammit. But how was she supposed to react when she slept with him and was forgotten and some other nameless woman did the same thing and received emeralds?

"Who you buy jewelry for is none of my business," she said. "I just hope the poor woman knows what she's letting herself in for."

"Oh, I think she knows," he said, smiling now.

"Amazing to me how many women are sucked into your orbit," she said.

"As I recall, you liked my orbit just fine."

She scowled at him. "I thought you said you didn't recall much at all."

"Oh, the memories are hazy, but they're there." He leaned in toward her and lowered his voice even further until it was no more than a sexy rumble that rolled along her spine. "Lightly tanned skin in the moonlight. The buzz of something electrical when we touched. The sigh of your breath."

He paused and Bella shivered.

"Care to refresh my memory further?"

Indignation rose up hot and hideous inside her. He was the most appalling male on the face of the planet. Yes, sexy. Yes, gorgeous. But absolutely zero moral center.

"Oh, yeah," she hissed at him with a fierce shake of her head, "that's gonna happen. You're actually standing here, buying emeralds for one conquest, while trying to line up another. I feel so sorry for whoever this woman is, if I knew her name, I'd find her and warn her about you."

He leaned back against the glass case, looking completely at ease while Bella's insides were twisting themselves into hard, tight knots.

"Trust me when I say she doesn't need warning," Jesse told her.

"Why, I'll bet she's sitting at home thinking you're something special and has zero idea that you're trying to snuggle up to me and—"

"Snuggle?" he interrupted with a wink. "Nothing wrong with a good snuggle."

She stopped and gaped at him. "God, you really are a pig, aren't you?"

"I don't think pigs snuggle. Of course, to a pig, it might seem like snuggling…"

"You're making a joke out of this." Bella cut him off. "And it isn't funny."

He sighed. "Come on, Bella. It was a little funny. Now, why don't you and I go have lunch so we can talk about this?"

"Not a chance," Bella said, taking a step back just for good measure. Despite the fact that she knew Jesse King was bad news, her body continued to respond to him. And what did that say about her, she wondered. He was the only man who had affected her like this.

"There is absolutely *nothing* that would convince me to repeat a mistake I've spent three years trying to block out of my memory." All right, a little lie. But she couldn't very well admit to him what that night had meant to her. Besides, now that she was getting to know him a little better, she was beginning to rethink those blurry memories of pleasure.

His smile slipped a little and a quick flash of irritation sparked in his eyes. "If you'd really been trying to block that night out of your mind, you wouldn't be so mad right now about me buying jewelry for another woman."

She hissed in a breath and when she spoke again, her voice was low and sizzled with fury. "Are you serious? Is your ego really that big?"

"Bella, if you'd just shut up for a second..."

"Shut up?" Her eyes went wide and her head jerked back as if he'd slapped her. She shot another quick look at Kevin and his customer as if to reassure herself that they were absorbed in their own discussion. "Shut up? I can't believe you just said that to me."

"Bella, if you'll let me talk," he said, irritation beginning to color his voice.

"Oh, you've said plenty," she told him, riding the wave of anger that was cresting inside, threatening to choke her. "You're standing here trying to charm me, all the while you're buying expensive jewelry for some poor, misguided woman who probably thinks you love her."

"I do."

She actually gasped. Stung. Hurt. Furious. Amazing that all those emotions could crowd inside her at once, each clamoring for recognition. Pain jangled through her with sharp, jagged edges and she wondered why. Bella hadn't thought she'd really cared one way or another about Jesse King, but hearing him admit to her that he loved another woman was just...awful.

She shouldn't care. It shouldn't matter. Bella hadn't seen him in three years. She didn't want him in her life.

But oh God, knowing that it would never happen hit her on a level she hadn't really expected. And that made her even more furious with him.

"You bastard."

"Hey," he said, smiling now, "of course I love her. She's a great woman. Funny, smart..."

"Mazel tov," she snapped and tried to walk past him. "Don't bother sending me an invitation to the wedding."

"Wedding's over."

"What?" That stopped her dead in her tracks. Had she really been fantasizing about a married man all this time? "You're *married?*"

Jesse laughed and finally Kevin and his customer turned to look at them curiously. After a moment or two, they went back to business, though Kevin still managed to keep one eye on them while he worked and Bella tried to get herself under control.

This was even worse than she'd thought.

"You're married?" she repeated it, because she just couldn't believe this.

"No, I'm not. She is."

Better? She wondered, or worse? She voted worse. "Well, that makes you a real hero, doesn't it? Buying jewelry for a married woman."

"Her husband will understand."

"Oh, sure he will."

"You don't believe me," he said, smiling, "but my cousin Travis knows that I'm nuts about his wife, Julie."

"Yeah, I'll bet he does—" Bella broke off when his words finally registered. All her air left her in a rush as she noticed his wide smile and the pure enjoyment shining in his eyes. Still a little stunned, she whispered, *"What?"*

He reached out, took her hand in his and moved his thumb over her skin in a caress meant to be soothing, but was instead firing up her nerve endings. Why did it have to be Jesse King who could electrify her entire body with a single touch?

As if he knew exactly what she was thinking, his blue eyes danced with amusement and something more…intimate. "The necklace and earrings are for my cousin Travis's wife, Julie."

Bella blinked, shook her head as if she hadn't heard him correctly and repeated, just for clarification, "Your cousin's wife?"

"Yep," Jesse said, one corner of his mouth lifting into a half grin and Bella knew he was enjoying himself. "She just had a baby. Their second. A boy this time. Their little girl, Katie, is almost two and Colin was born a month ago."

"So you bought her emeralds," Bella said, feeling the last of her anger fade away to be replaced by a swell of something that felt a lot like tenderness. Which was a far more dangerous emotion to be entertaining about Jesse King.

"I did," he said. "She has green eyes, and Travis is always buying her emeralds, so when I saw that necklace here, I couldn't resist."

He bought an expensive necklace for his cousin's wife. Why did knowing that make Bella's heart soften toward him? Because he was close to his family. Clearly appreciated them. And she'd lived most of her life alone, so family was something of an elusive dream for her.

A small curl of envy wound through her for Julie King. Not only did she have a husband who loved her and two children, but she had cousins who cared enough to buy her something special to celebrate the birth of her child.

"So," he asked quietly, "am I still a pig?"

"Probably," Bella said on a sigh, "but not about this, obviously."

"You sound disappointed."

"No," Bella admitted, meeting his gaze squarely, "just confused."

"Well, now," Jesse said, still giving her that amazing smile of his, "I've gotta say, I consider that a step in the right direction."

"How's that?"

"Confusion means you're no longer so sure that I'm the devil incarnate and that means just maybe you're willing to take a chance."

Her heartbeat quickened and her stomach did a slow roll and spin. Darn it, her body was working against her. Bella knew, logically, that she should stay very far away from Jesse King. She'd already been burned once, so wouldn't it be the height of stupidity to stand in line to be burned again?

Yet…he was buying his cousin's wife emeralds. He was close enough to his family that he not only wanted to do something special for the new mom, but it felt right to him to do it. That said something about him, too, didn't it?

Life had been a lot easier when she had just hated him.

"What kind of chance?" she finally asked.

That smile of his brightened even further. "How about you give me the opportunity to take you around my offices. Show you I'm not the CEO of the evil empire that you think I am."

"Why do you care what I think?" she asked, instead of answering his question.

He studied her for a long minute before admitting, "I'm not sure, but I do."

"That's honest anyway."

"I'm just that kind of guy."

"Hmm. That's yet to be seen," Bella said softly, "but I'll take the tour of King Beach."

"That's good enough for now," he said. "How about in an hour?"

"Fine," she said, the fight gone out of her as her mind and heart and body all struggled to make sense of this latest insight into Jesse King.

"Okay. See you then." He walked out of Kevin's shop without a backward glance, leaving Bella feeling more confused than ever.

Five

Jesse waited for Bella on the sidewalk outside King Beach. For some weird reason, he felt almost like a teenager on a first date. Which was beyond stupid. Since not only wasn't this a date, but he'd already slept with Bella. So it wasn't as if this was the first time he would ever be alone with her.

Late-afternoon sunlight poured down on him from a brilliant blue sky. Traffic down Main Street was light, but the sidewalks were filled with people strolling in and out of the shops in the newly rehabbed business district. Everyone in Morgan Beach was happy with what he'd done there. Everyone but the one woman he was interested in.

Were the fates finally getting back at him? His entire

life, women had come easily to him. Now, there was Bella. A woman whose memory had haunted him for three years and now that he'd found her again she wanted nothing to do with him. Even worse, she had something going on with that Kevin guy. But what? he wondered. Was she in love with the other man?

Scowling at the thought, Jesse told himself it didn't matter. Whatever she felt for someone else could be dealt with. He wanted Bella and Jesse King didn't lose. Ever.

"Well, you look fierce."

He snapped out of his thoughts and looked down into chocolate-brown eyes. She'd slipped up on him unnoticed and he couldn't figure out how. Her scent alone should have alerted him. It was a blend of flowers and spice that somehow reminded him of summer nights. Well, *one* summer night in particular.

"Sorry," he said, smiling at her. "Just thinking."

"Couldn't have been happy thoughts."

"You might be surprised," he said and took her arm, turning her toward the front door of King Beach headquarters. When he took a step forward though, she didn't move. Turning to look down at her again, he asked, "What's the problem?"

She frowned, chewed at her bottom lip and finally admitted, "I feel as if I'm walking into enemy territory."

"Expecting an ambush?"

She whipped her long, thick, brown hair out of her way and stared up at him. "Honestly, I don't know what to expect."

"Well, then," Jesse said, enjoying her nervousness a bit, "let's get started and satisfy your curiosity."

He led her through the door and paused just inside the threshold. A receptionist's desk sat just opposite the door and the woman seated there was busily answering a phone that rang incessantly. Smiling at the woman, Jesse walked past her to the elevator bank, pushed the button and waited, still holding on to Bella as if he were worried that she'd bolt.

But she didn't. She stood there with an expression that made him think of martyrs about to be burned at the stake. He wished she would smile. Amazing how this one badly dressed woman could get to him so easily.

Over the last few days though, his mind had been filling in some blanks. Now that he knew who his mystery woman was, his memory of that night three years ago was becoming clearer. He could see her face now, as she'd looked in the moonlight. He could hear her voice, sighing. And he damn well remembered that she hadn't dressed like a Hungarian peasant back in the day. So he couldn't help wondering why she was dressing that way now.

Only one way to find out. "So, want to tell me why you wear those shapeless clothes?"

"Excuse me?" She turned her face up to his.

He waved one hand to encompass her loose, pale green shirt and flowing, floor-length yellow skirt. Maybe he shouldn't have said anything. After all, he was trying to charm and seduce her, not piss her off further.

But dammit, he'd seen the body she had hidden underneath all that fabric and he couldn't understand why she was so determined to disguise it. Especially, he thought, since she hadn't before. He distinctly remembered her wearing faded jeans and a low-necked, body-hugging T-shirt.

She flushed and Jesse was charmed. He couldn't remember the last time he'd seen a woman blush. But her one moment of embarrassment was gone an instant later. Her dark eyes flashed as she said, "Not that it's any of your business, but I like wearing natural fabrics."

He should have backed off, but couldn't help himself. "Natural, sure. But why…" He shook his head, clearly baffled.

The elevator chimed, the doors hissed open and Bella stepped inside. Turning around sharply, she lifted her chin, glared at him and said, "I stopped wearing form-fitting clothes three years ago when I discovered it attracted men who were interested in only one thing."

In the harsh, overhead glare of the fluorescent lights, she looked ferocious and proud. Like a female Viking. And Jesse felt a shot of admiration rip through him, along with a quick flash of shame. Because of *him,* she was dressing like a refugee from a rag factory? She was hiding that glorious body because he'd slept with her and disappeared from her life?

Vaguely disgusted with himself, he walked into the elevator beside her and punched the second-floor button. Strange, but until this moment, he'd never before considered what a woman thought of him after their time together was over. He'd always enjoyed himself, made sure his lady of the moment had a good time and then he'd moved on.

Uneasiness settled over him as he wondered how many other women he might have left wounded in his wake. He'd never thought of himself as a hurting women kind of guy. Hell, he *liked* women. But now…he had to wonder.

Still, he felt compelled to say something, so he said, "I don't think your strategy's working."

"Really?" she asked, her voice just carrying over the distantly annoying Muzak playing over the speakers. "I haven't been bothered by unwanted men in three years."

He found that hard to believe. "Then the men in this town are blind or extremely shortsighted and probably stupid to boot, so you're better off without them."

"Is that right?" She glanced up at him from beneath long, dark lashes.

"Damn straight," he told her, meeting her gaze squarely. Fine. He'd messed up. But that was in the past. And she might as well know that whatever she was wearing, she got to him on levels no one else ever had.

"The clothes are ugly, I grant you. But they don't disguise your eyes. Or your mouth." He lifted one hand and smoothed the pad of his thumb over her bottom lip. She pulled her head back quickly, and he smiled, shaking his head. "And even if you'd been dressed like this three years ago… I still would have noticed you."

She blinked at him, obviously surprised, and Jesse felt like a jerk. For the first time in his life, he was faced with a woman he'd used and walked away from. And for the first time in his life, he regretted what he'd done. A new experience for him. And not an entirely comfortable one.

The elevator opened, sparing them both from having to continue the conversation. A buzz of activity and conversation rolled toward them in a thick wave and Jesse smiled. He may not have started out as a businessman, but he certainly enjoyed the sights and sounds of his success. He knew all too well that it was because of him that this company was growing beyond all imaginings. And he had a real sense of pride in what he'd accomplished in a few short years.

"Come on, Bella," he said, holding out one hand toward her and smiling. "Let me show you around the enemy camp."

She glanced from him to the room and back again before reluctantly slipping her hand into his and following him out into the middle of organized chaos. Phones were ringing, printers were hissing as they shot sheet after sheet of paper onto trays and the low rumble of dozens of conversations almost sounded like the roar of the ocean.

He walked her through King Beach like a king overseeing his estate. He made sure she saw all the latest technology and the swarms of people he had handling sales, marketing and publicity. Really getting into his spiel, Jesse pointed out the wall maps with the locations of the hundreds of King Beach stores and turned to bask in her admiration.

But Bella wasn't watching him or his presentation.

Instead, she was marching up and down the aisles, peeking into cubicles and rummaging in trash cans.

"What are you doing?" he asked, coming up behind her.

She straightened, spun around and faced him, holding an empty soda can aloft as if it were a gold nugget she'd scraped out of the earth. "Look at this! You don't even *recycle!*"

A muffled snort of laughter came from the guy whose cubicle had been invaded, but one steely look from Jesse ended his amusement fast. Everything he'd shown her. Everything he'd done to try to impress her hadn't meant a thing. No, she focused on empty soda cans. He admired her passion. She practically vibrated with it, and he wanted nothing more than to see it up close and personal again. Hell, there she stood, telling him off and his body was more than ready for her. Was it any wonder she fascinated him?

"Sure we recycle, Bella," he said, his voice patient. He shook his head and looked into her eyes, fired now with righteous indignation. "It's just not done up here. The janitorial staff handles it every night."

"Of course they do," she mumbled, dropping the can back into the trash, then glaring at him. "You hire someone to do the right thing for you rather than making the effort to do it yourself."

"What?"

"You heard me," she said, her voice low, but vehement. "You don't care what your company does as long as there's a healthy bottom line. You don't even ask your employees to recycle. How hard would it be to put *two* trash cans into every cubicle? Is it really so difficult to take personal responsibility for what your company produces?"

The resident of the cubicle hunched his shoulders, lowered his head and started typing, actively trying to ignore both of them. Jesse shook his head again, took Bella's arm and drew her out of the cubicle. He was not going to defend himself to her in front of his employees.

When they were far enough away from curious ears, he said, "In case you hadn't noticed, those cubicles are too small to cram much more into them."

"Easy excuse."

"What does it matter how the recycling gets done as long as it is done?"

"It's the principle of the thing," she muttered, folding her arms beneath her breasts and unintentionally, he was sure, outlining them nicely.

"The principle. So it's not recycling. It's having *me* recycle."

She frowned.

"I hire people to do that job."

"Hmph."

"Okay," Jesse said, leaning in closer to her, bending low so that he could look directly into her eyes. "Would it make you feel better if I fired the entire janitorial staff and did it all myself? Would that make the world a better place for you, Bella? Putting twenty people out of work? Does that help the environment?"

She was scowling now and her mouth was working

as if there were words locked behind her grimly closed lips fighting to get out. But after a few long seconds, her shoulders slumped, her mouth relaxed and she huffed out a breath. "All right, I suppose I can see your point."

Jesse grinned. She might be a hard case, but she could admit when she was wrong, which was more than he could say for a lot of people. She didn't look at all happy about seeing his point, but that didn't matter. She *had* seen it.

"I think I'm having a moment, here. I've just scored a point off Bella Cruz."

She snorted.

He held up a hand, grinned even more broadly and said, "Wait. Not finished relishing. I want to enjoy the glory of this small victory." Seconds ticked past, then with a deep breath said, "Okay, I'm done."

"Is everything a joke to you?" she asked, staring up at him.

"Who said I was joking?" Jesse teased. "Getting you to admit that I have a point about *anything* is well worth celebrating."

She rolled her eyes, but her lips twitched and Jesse felt as if he'd scored another victory.

"Now," he said, taking her hand in his, "how about finishing the tour?"

Her hand lay limply in his for a brief moment, then her fingers curled around his and this time, he kept his smile to himself. She walked beside him, spoke to a few of the people answering phones and Jesse watched as she charmed everyone. Apparently, his mystery woman had plenty of personality—she just wasn't using it on him.

Clearly, she didn't trust herself to relax around him. But that was fine with him. He didn't want her relaxed—he wanted her hot and bothered and poised on the edge of sexual heat. Then he wanted to take her over that edge.

Oh, yeah, he thought. He was going to have Bella again. He was going to wine her, dine her and seduce her until she begged him to take over her business and make her a millionaire. And once the business end of things was taken care of, he told himself, they'd go from there. Once she was a part of King Beach, it would be better for her. Better for him. Better for everyone.

He stood to one side as Bella chatted with a couple of the secretaries. They were both talking about her swimwear and how they wished they could find good suits like that everywhere. Say, for example, at King Beach. Jesse frowned a little to hear even his own employees saying that his company wasn't meeting the demands of all the consumers. But that only helped to convince him that the decision to absorb Bella's company into his own was the right one.

As if he'd heard Jesse's thoughts, Dave Michaels walked up, a stack of folders caught under one arm and an eager expression of welcome on his face. "Bella," he said, giving Jesse a nod of greeting, "we're delighted to have you here. Jesse told me he was going to give you a tour. Hope you don't mind if I call you Bella."

"Not at all," she said, stepping away from the two

women she'd been talking to as they went back to work. "This is all very...impressive."

She said *impressive,* but Jesse told himself she didn't sound impressed. She sounded just a little bit disgusted.

"Well, we're big and we're growing," Dave said, glee lacing his voice. "Which is just one of the reasons I'm glad you're here. As you know, King Beach doesn't really cater to women—"

Jesse's ears perked up and he shook his head wildly from behind Bella, hoping to head the man off. It wasn't time yet to hit her with the information that they were interested in buying out Bella's Beachwear. And when it *was* the right moment, Jesse intended to be the one to do the telling. Bella was a special case. She wasn't some ordinary CEO of a big company who would welcome a takeover if the money were right. He had to approach her cautiously or the whole thing would blow up in his face.

Dave caught the frantic motion and stopped himself midsentence. "But I have to tell you," he said, changing the subject smoothly, "my wife bought a bathing suit from you that she can't stop raving about."

"Isn't that nice?" Bella beamed at him as if the man had just presented her with a bouquet of roses. "I hope she comes back."

"Oh, she will. She's bringing her sisters to your shop next week," Dave assured her. "Connie's been bragging about your store so much, all three of them have insisted on visiting Bella's."

"Thank you, I'm always glad to hear about a satisfied customer."

"Yes, aren't we all," Jesse muttered, and jerked his head, silently telling Dave to take a hike.

Dave got the message. "Right. Well, I've got a few calls to make, so I'd better let you get on with your tour. Nice to see you here, Bella. Hope we see you again soon."

Bella watched him go, then turned to look at Jesse. "I like your friend."

"But not me," he added for her.

"Does it matter?" she asked and her voice was almost lost in the bustle of the office.

Yeah, it mattered. He wasn't sure why and he didn't like acknowledging the fact, even to himself. So he for damn sure wasn't going to let her know how he felt. That woman had enough power over him already.

"Let me show you my office," he said instead.

"Oh, Mr. King," a woman called out as she hurried up to meet them. "We've just heard back on the surfing exhibition plans. The city's approved everything and your guests have all agreed to take part."

"Good news, Sue," Jesse said, catching the gleam of curiosity in Bella's eyes. "Put a call in to Wiki, will you? Tell him I'll be getting in touch with him by tomorrow."

"Will do." The woman hurried off, the tap of her heels swallowed by the bustling noise of the busy office.

"Wiki?" Bella asked as Jesse took her arm and steered her toward his office at the back of the long, wide room.

"Danny Wikiloa," he said, opening the door for her. Once inside, he closed the door before adding, "He's a professional surfer. We competed against each other for years.

He's coming into town in two weeks for the exhibition. Doing it as a favor to me, actually, since he's retired, too."

"The exhibition," she murmured. "Everyone in town has been talking about it for days."

He stuffed both hands into his jeans pockets as he watched her wander the perimeter of his office. She noticed everything, pausing to look at the framed photos of different beaches. She hardly glanced at his surfing trophies, which stung a bit, but she seemed fascinated by the one wall where photos of his family were hanging.

"It's going to be fun," he said, walking over to join her. "Ten of the world's best surfers giving a one-day exhibition."

"You miss it, don't you? The competition, I mean."

He hadn't really admitted it to anyone else, but, "Yeah, I do. I like winning."

She nodded. "Not surprising. The whole King family is like that, aren't they?"

"Pretty much," he said and turned his back on the family photos so he could look instead at Bella. "We enjoy competing and we don't lose gracefully."

She tipped her head to one side, looked at him and said, "You can't always win."

"Don't see why not."

"You really don't, do you?"

"Nope," he told her and took the single step separating them. Standing alongside her, he looked up at the family photos and waved one hand at them. "Not a single one of those people is the type to settle for second place."

"Sometimes you don't have a choice," Bella said softly.

"There's always a choice, Bella." Jesse glanced at one familiar face and then another as he said, "The King family decided a long time ago that the only people who lose are the ones who expect to. We expect to win, so we do."

"Easy as that?"

He looked down at her and found her staring up at him. Those chocolate-brown eyes of hers looked deep and dark and filled with secrets. Secrets he wanted to know. To share. Lifting one hand, he cupped her cheek and said, "I never said it was easy. But winning shouldn't be. Takes all the fun out of it if everyone could do it."

"And fun's important to you, too," she said, stepping back, away from his touch, away from *him.*

"Should be important to everyone," he said, his palm still tingling from the touch of her skin against his. "What's life if you don't enjoy it? Hell, why do *anything* if you don't enjoy it?"

"And you enjoy what you do now?"

"Yeah," he said with a shrug. "I didn't think I would, you know. Never planned to be the suit-wearing guy, Mr. Businessman. But I'm good at it."

She looked toward the closed office door and the busy office beyond. "Yes, I guess you are."

"See, I'm enjoying this. We're agreeing on things."

"Don't get used to it," she told him wryly.

"Why not? We could make a great team, Bella."

She laughed a little. "We're so not a team, Jesse."

This was it, he thought. The moment. Time to slide an offer in here while she was still impressed by her tour. While she still liked him a little. It struck him then that he'd never had to work so hard to get a woman to like him. "We could be. Think about it. King Beach. Bella's Beachwear. A match made in heaven."

She stilled, slid an uneasy look at him and asked, "What kind of match?"

"Well, I wasn't going to bring this up so soon, but I don't like waiting, either. So I'll get right to it." He walked to his desk and leaned back against it. Through the wide window behind him, the sun splashed down on the view of Morgan Beach and the ocean stretching out to the horizon. "I want to buy Bella's Beachwear."

Six

"No." Bella blurted the word out instinctively.

"Jeez." He came up off the desk and took a step toward her. "At least let me finish my sentence."

"No need to, I'm not for sale." She should have known. Should have guessed that he was softening her up for something. She'd allowed herself to relax around him. All right, she'd actually been enjoying herself. The touch of his hand, that wicked smile of his, the way he seemed to focus so intently on her. All that had combined to weaken her defenses and now she was going to pay.

"I'm not trying to buy *you,* Bella. Just your business."

"That's what you don't get, Jesse. I *am* my business." Irritated, hurt and just a little angry at herself for walking into this mess, she continued, "You want to buy my swimwear, but to you it's just that. Bathing suits. Stick them on a rack, sell them to the masses."

Both his eyebrows rose. "There's something wrong with selling your product to people who want it?"

"No, but I'm not interested in the quick, easy sale." She took a deep breath, fisted her hands at her sides and tried once again to get through his hard head. "I'm interested in the *whole* woman. Helping ordinary women build their self-esteem. *You're* interested in making the young and skinny feel pretty. Well, guess what, they already do."

"Bella, I know you think I want to change what you do, but you couldn't be more wrong." He threw both hands up, then let them fall to his thighs. "I've been resisting selling women's stuff for years because how the hell do I know what women want to wear? Everything I stock I personally believe in. That's the reason I want *you* to be a part of King Beach. Because *you* believe in your stuff the way I believe in mine."

"It's not 'stuff.'"

He laughed and Bella simmered.

"I get it, I get it. Your line is not interchangeable with department store swimsuits."

"I'm not looking to be bought out or rolled over or absorbed by King Beach. You can't buy me up like you did this city, Jesse. I won't let you ruin the thing I love just for the sake of business."

"So you have something against becoming a millionaire?" he countered. "Because I promise you, join me and that's what you'll be."

For just one, brief, electrifying moment, she actually considered his offer and thought about what it would mean to her to be financially independent. She could buy her little house from Kevin. She could donate all the money she wanted to the different charities that had always tugged at her heart. She could… Bella stopped, gasped and accused, "You're the devil."

He grinned. "Good. That means you're thinking about it."

"I did, for about thirty seconds."

"That's a start."

"No," Bella insisted. "It's not. I'm not set up for large-scale production. I'm a cottage industry and I like it that way. I know my weavers, my seamstresses. I personally choose fabrics, design styles. The women who work for me care as much about the product as I do. We're making a statement."

"Yes, but do you have to make it *poor?*" He grinned and said, "Think about this. You align with King Beach and you'll be creating more jobs. Better money for your weavers and seamstresses. We'll be able to use them, I know. Hell, they can probably teach the pros a thing or two."

"They *are* pros," she told him.

"I'm sure. But on a much smaller scale," he said. "Don't you see, Bella? Signing with me will get you and your company even more."

"I know you want my shop, but I'm not turning my business over to you."

"I don't just want your business, Bella," he said. "I want *you.*"

Oh God. A quick blast of something hot, delicious and practically mind-numbing shot through her. He wanted her. Jesse King wanted Bella Cruz. Did he mean that? And what exactly *did* he mean? Want? Want how? For how long? In what way? Oh God. Her stomach was a mess and in a split second, her mind took off on dozens of wild, crazy tangents that splintered again and again, teasing her with possibilities. Until he spoke again and shattered them all.

"I want you to run the business for us. You'll still be designing, you'll still have the final say in everything related to Bella's Beachwear—"

Just like that, the heat she'd been feeling drained away to be replaced by a chill snaking along her spine. Okay, fine. He didn't want *her.* He wanted her to work with him. For him. So much for dazzling daydreams, born to die within a few seconds of birth.

She had to stop setting herself up for disappointment. Jesse wasn't even on the same wavelength, and wishing it were different wasn't going to change a thing.

"This was your plan from the beginning, wasn't it?" she asked, and hoped she didn't sound as depressed as she felt at the moment. "All of your teasing and flirting was designed to get me off guard."

"That depends. Are you?"

She ignored that little quip. "All your talk about how King Beach doesn't cater to women was just that. Talk. You've been planning on trying to take me over from the very start."

"Considered it, yes. The day of the photo shoot

opened my eyes. But you've only got yourself to blame for that," he added, standing up straight and looking at her through eyes as blue as the sea. "You're the one who showed me what a difference your swimwear could make on a woman's body. You're the one who laid it all out for me. Is it my fault you started me thinking?"

She never should have done it, she thought now. Never should have put on one of her own suits. Never should have risen to his challenge just because she'd wanted to prove him wrong. She'd wanted to show off. And all that maneuver had done was dig her a deeper hole.

"It doesn't matter," she said, shaking her head as she watched him. "Nothing's changed. I haven't changed. I'm still not interested. Do you think you're the first company to try to buy me out? You're not. And you probably won't be the last. But I'm not selling, Jesse. This time, you lose."

"God, you're stubborn."

"I was just thinking the same thing about you," she countered and let the simmering fury inside bubble and boil. He was standing there smiling. As if he could change her opinion if he just smiled long enough. Did that technique work with most women? Of course it did. He probably never heard the word *no*.

Had to be a King thing.

"It's in your blood, isn't it?" she asked, voicing her thoughts. "You and every other member of the King family. You've always gotten what you wanted, so you expect nothing less. You've lived a charmed life," she told him. "Not many people do."

Instantly, he shifted position a bit, obviously uncomfortable with the turn of the conversation. "Okay, I grant you that. But if you think the King cousins were raised to be lazy or indulged or pampered, you've got us all wrong."

"Really." She glanced at the wall of family photos again and said, "None of these people look like they've had a rough life."

Jesse looked up, and pointed at one of them. "That's my brother, Justice."

Bella studied the photo. A gorgeous man with light brown hair, blue eyes narrowed, squinting at the sun. Justice King stood in an open field, arms folded across his chest, cowboy hat pulled low over his forehead. "Interesting name."

"My dad had just won a huge lawsuit the day he was born. Somehow he convinced mom that *Justice* was a perfectly reasonable name."

"Winning again."

"That's right," he said, smiling. "But let me tell you about Justice and the life of the pampered rich." Jesse eased down to sit on the arm of a brown leather chair. Looking up at her, he said, "Justice has a ranch about an hour from here. He's up at dawn every morning, checking his herds and his fences and the weather report. I swear he lives by the Weather Channel. As if the weather changes that much in southern California." Shaking his head, he laughed ruefully. "Our cousin Adam has a ranch too, farther north. He raises horses. Justice raises organically fed beef cattle. And grows acres of hay. He works twice as hard as any of his cowboys and wouldn't know how to be pampered if somebody paid him to try."

Bella frowned thoughtfully. "And that one?"

Jesse looked. "Ah, cousin Travis. He with the beautiful wife who loves emeralds." He pointed to a few other framed photos. "Those are his brothers, Jackson and Adam, with their wives, Casey and Gina. They've got kids, too. Two girls each. And I hear Gina's pregnant again." Getting into it now, he touched another photo of two smiling men. "This one is cousin Rico and his brother Nick at Rico's hotel in Mexico. For some reason their other brothers weren't around on that trip. And that's Nathan and Garret at some aunt's wedding. Their brothers Chance and Nash and Kieran are the three in that picture and—"

"How many of you are there?" she asked, amazement coloring her tone.

"Dozens and dozens. And probably more out there we haven't met!" Jesse laughed, obviously enjoying himself. "You can't kick a rock in California without turning up a King."

"It's…"

"Too much?" he offered, still smiling. "Way too many Kings running around?"

"It's wonderful," she finally said, and her voice was a little poignant. A minute or so ago, she'd been furious with him, trying to steamroll her into giving up the most important thing in the world to her, her business.

Now that anger was pretty much gone, swamped by

a tide of envy so thick she could barely breathe. She couldn't even imagine what it would be like to have so much family. As a kid, she'd hungered for parents. Or for a single brother or sister. Someone to whom she was linked. Jesse really *was* rich and she wondered if he even realized that the King family's real wealth wasn't in banks, but in each other.

Jesse's smile faded. "Are you okay?"

She nodded and pointed to another photo. She didn't want to talk about herself. "Who's that?"

"My eldest brother, Jefferson. He runs the King Studios. Makes movies and runs himself ragged because he doesn't trust anyone but himself to handle the details."

Jefferson King's photo made him look like a dangerous man. He was wearing a white shirt, black slacks and giving the camera a hard glare, as if he resented being captured on film.

"How many brothers do you have?" Her voice was a whisper now and even she heard the yearning in it.

Softly now, he answered, "Three."

"Three brothers. And so many cousins…who is he?" she asked. "The marine?"

Jesse grinned even more broadly. "My brother Jericho. Now *there's* a pampered, lazy rich guy. A gunnery sergeant. Didn't want to be an officer. Said he'd rather serve with *real* marines. He's done two tours overseas," Jesse said and frowned when he added, "and he's about to be shipped out again."

Bella sighed, folded her arms beneath her breasts and looked at the man who still filled far too much of her thoughts. He wasn't what she'd expected. His whole *family* wasn't what she'd expected. Hardworking ranchers. Marines. And apparently they were all so close that it felt natural for Jesse to hang family photos in his office.

She envied him that connection. That solid base with so much family. Lives intertwined, bonds strengthened by years of love. What must it be like, she wondered, to have so much? To know that it was simply *there* whenever you needed it?

"Bella? You okay?"

"Yes," she said and looked at him. His blue eyes were narrowed on her and he was watching her as a soldier might keep a wary eye on a live grenade. "You just…surprised me, that's all."

"Why? Because I have a family?"

"No, because you love them so much."

"It surprises you to know that I love my family?" His features were as taut as his voice.

"You just never seemed…" She broke off, shook her head and said, "Never mind. It was nothing."

"Uh-huh," he said, moving in closer to her. "Well, if these pictures impressed you, you should know I have more."

She laughed shortly. "More?"

"Lots more pictures of everyone at home," he said, smiling again. "I ran out of wall space in here."

"This isn't fair," she said, looking from him to all the photos.

"What?"

"I thought I had you pegged," she admitted. "A

modern-day robber baron stomping his way through life, taking what he wanted and making no apologies."

"You weren't completely wrong," he said, "I do go after what I want and I don't let anybody stop me." He moved in even closer until all that separated them was an inch or two of space and Bella's own firm resolve.

Which was weakening, darn it.

She felt the heat of him sliding off his body, reaching for her, and it was so tempting to stand her ground, let him close that last inch or two of space so she could feel his tall, lean body pressed against her. Her memories of their one night together were still so vivid, it was all she could do to keep from flinging herself at him. But if she did that, then she'd be lost and she knew it. So she did the only thing she could. She stepped back—mentally and physically.

He sighed. "You don't have to be afraid of me, Bella."

"I'm not. Afraid I mean. Just…cautious."

"Cautious is okay," he allowed, giving her a small, wicked smile. "It just means that you take your time. But once you're sure of your footing, you'll move ahead."

She knew what he was talking about. There wasn't much subtext there. He wanted her. And oh God, she wanted him, too. But she'd wanted him three years ago, too. And what had that gotten her? One night of glory and three years of misery. Was she really ready to set herself up for that kind of pain again?

Jesse King wasn't the "forever" kind of guy. Bella wasn't the "temporary" kind of girl. So never the twain should meet.

"Why don't you go to dinner with me?"

"What?" Okay, that offer had come out of nowhere.

"Dinner," he repeated. "Usually considered the last meal of the day?"

His smile really was a weapon all its own. At least, for her, it was. "I don't know if that's a good idea."

"It's a great idea," he said, and closed the distance separating them again. "Look, you've been on a tour of the business. You've seen for yourself that the place isn't a sweatshop. Happy, well-paid employees, I must be a halfway decent boss, yes?"

"Yes…"

"And I'm not that hard to spend time with, am I?"

"No…"

"So we have a meal. We talk. We…"

"Jesse, I'm still not going to sell my business to you."

He cut her off, laid both hands on her shoulders and she felt the heat of his skin seeping through the fabric of her shirt and down, deep into her bones.

"I'm not talking about the business right now. I want you, Bella. I've wanted you for three years." His gaze moved over her like a warm caress. "Hell, I've *dreamed* of you for three years. You want me, too. I can feel it every time we're together."

"I don't always do what I want," she told him, and kept thinking, *Strong, Bella. Be tough. Be strong. Don't give in.* Unfortunately, her body wasn't listening.

"You should," he said with a quick grin. "But that's a talk for another time. Right now, I've got a deal for you."

Uh-oh. Making deals with a man who refused to

lose could never be considered a good idea. Warily, she asked, "What kind of deal?"

"A simple one. Perfect for both of us." He stroked his palms up and down her arms and the friction he caused was enough to kindle a sort of sweeping wildfire that began licking at her insides. "You think you know me, right?"

"All too well," she said.

He nodded. "Well, I think you're wrong and I'm willing to bet on it. If I manage to show you something about me that truly shocks you, we have sex. Again."

That one, three-letter word—*sex*—conjured up so many different emotions and needs, she could hardly draw a breath for the strangling effect on her lungs. "Now just a minute—"

"Come on, Bella. You've said yourself that you know exactly what kind of guy I am."

"Yes, but—" She waved a hand at the wall of family photos. "You've already surprised me there."

"Because I love my family," he said, as if he still couldn't believe that. "But I'm not talking about a surprise. I'm talking about *shock.* If I can really shock you, you have sex with me. Again."

"Stop saying *again.*"

He grinned. "No reason to pretend you're insulted or anything," he pointed out a second later. "We've already had each other once. I'm just saying, it'd be nice to have each other *again.*"

"You're doing that on purpose. Reminding me."

"Damn straight. Is it working?"

Yes, she almost shrieked. She was so out of her element here, Bella thought. Jesse King was a Major League Flirter. He could play this game in his sleep—probably did—where Bella was just lost. She didn't do the flirting thing. She was much more the honesty-is-the-best-policy type. Which probably explained the dearth of dates in her life.

Taking a deep breath, she met his gaze squarely, determined not to let him see just how rattled she actually was. But he'd know how crazy he was making her if she were too afraid to accept his deal, wouldn't he? She gave an inward sigh. "This deal. I know what happens if I lose. What do I get if I win?"

One eyebrow lifted and his mouth curved into a smile. "If I fail to shock you completely—and you've got to be honest—then I'll quit bugging you about buying your business."

Well. She hadn't expected that. This was too easy, Bella thought, watching him as he stood there staring at her with a smug smirk on his face. Clearly, he believed he would win this bet easily. But then, that was a part of who he was, wasn't it?

Hadn't he just told her that Kings never expect to lose?

And how satisfying would it be for her to knock him off his feet, so to speak? To beat him at the very deal *he'd* proposed? Oh, that would be sweet. The chance at doing just that was too tantalizing to turn down. Besides, he couldn't possibly shock her.

She knew exactly who Jesse King was.

"Okay," she said suddenly, before she could change

her mind, or listen to the outraged, rational screams rattling through her brain. "You're on. It's a deal."

"Friday night. Dinner and the bet."

She nodded. "Friday." Then she lifted her chin, held out her hand and waited.

"You want me to shake your hand?" he asked, glancing down briefly at her outstretched palm.

"Well, yes."

"Well," he countered, *"no."*

Then he caught her hand in his, pulled her in close and wrapped his arms around her. She was pressed so tightly to him, she felt every lean, muscular contour of his body—not to mention one specific part that left her no doubt as to just how he was feeling about her at the moment.

Bella looked up, met his gaze and held her breath as he lowered his head. The moment his lips met hers, everything stopped. Time screeched to a halt. The world probably stopped spinning on its axis. She knew for sure that she'd stopped breathing.

And more important, she didn't care.

Every cell in Bella's body leaped into life. Her blood rushed through her veins like a fiery flood. Her skin hummed. Her heart pounded frantically in her chest.

His mouth took hers in a hard, hot kiss that sizzled throughout her system like an out-of-control fireworks display. She felt alive and tingly and expectant. His tongue tangled with hers and heat dived through her, scalding everything she was, dragging her down, down into a kind of vortex where nothing was as it should be and everything shone with possibilities.

He gave her hunger and fed it.

He gave her passion and stoked it.

He gave her want and nurtured it.

Bella clung to him, pressing her body into his, relishing his hard, broad chest aligned with hers, loving the feel of that rigid proof of his desire for her pushing against her body. And while her brain shut down and her body sang, all Bella could think was, God help her if she really lost that bargain they'd just made.

Seven

For the next few days, Bella tried to put Jesse King and that kiss out of her mind. Which wasn't easy. Heck, the night she'd spent with him three years ago was still fresh in her mind. Having this latest example of his kissing prowess burned into her brain made it twice as hard to keep her mind from straying to him.

Still, if she kept busy, that helped. It was all the downtime, like sleeping, showering, washing dishes, taking a walk on the beach or even watching TV that was getting to her. The moment her brain had a free second, it leaped into thoughts of Jesse.

And her body wasn't far behind.

She'd almost been able to convince herself over the years that Jesse's kisses hadn't been *that* great. That the feel of his skin under her hands hadn't really felt like a slow burn. That his body wasn't actually that buff.

But a few short minutes alone in his office with him had shot down those little attempts at self-deception. Jesse was every bit as amazing as he had been three years ago. Her skin was still humming. And now that it was Friday, it was time to make good on the deal she'd made with him. Tonight, they'd have dinner. And if he managed to really shock her, they'd be having sex for dessert.

Oh, this was so not a good thing.

"Bella?" A voice called out from the dressing room and she walked toward the back of the store.

Desperately grateful for the distraction, Bella asked, "Do you need something?"

A blonde with big blue eyes poked her head up over the dressing-room door and grinned. "I need a smaller size in the silver swimsuit."

Bella laughed. "Didn't I tell you?"

The woman was a new customer and, like everyone else who came into her shop for the first time, she hadn't believed Bella when she'd advised that a well-made swimsuit would fit far differently than she was used to.

"I can't believe it," the blonde said, "but yeah, you were right."

"I'll be right back with a smaller size."

"Woo hoo, do I love hearing *that,*" the woman said with a laugh.

Bella passed three other women looking through the racks of suits, sarongs and wraps as she headed for the hip-hugger bikini section. There she flipped through the suits hung on short plastic hangers until she found the silver mesh suit in a size 10. Smiling, she walked back to her customer, handed it over and went back to the front of the store.

September was generally a slower month than usual. She had plenty of walk-in business during the summer months, but by September, summer was ending and only the hard-core sun worshippers were out in abundance. Of course, she still had plenty of business from the female surfers in town.

When the door opened, she sent a smile of welcome, only to bite it back at the last minute. Jesse King strolled in, looking completely at home. He paused on the threshold, took a look around and smiled at her customers before focusing his attention on Bella.

God, she hated to admit what just seeing him could do to her. He was wearing his own sportswear, a red polo shirt with a collar and the KB logo in gold on the left breast, along with a pair of khaki slacks and brown suede boots. His dark blond hair was wind-ruffled and the sun-carved crinkles at the corners of his eyes deepened as he smiled.

"Morning, ladies," he said, as he headed across the store toward Bella.

"Oh my God! That's Jesse King," someone muttered and a soft giggle followed the declaration.

Naturally, he heard, and his grin widened.

Great, Bella thought. He was going to turn *her* customers into *his* groupies. She sensed more than saw the women in the store staring at him and she wanted to tell them all to turn off their hormones. But that would be like setting a filet mignon down in front of a hungry man and telling him not to eat it. An exercise in utter futility.

"Bella," he said, flattening his palms on the glass counter. Then he lowered his voice until it was just a rumble of sound. "Good to see you again. Miss me?"

"No." *Yes.* He'd stayed away from her for three days. No doubt he'd done it deliberately to drive her nuts. Well, it wasn't working! Oh, she told herself, of course it was working.

He smiled as if he'd heard that stray thought from her sex-starved hormones.

"I missed you," he said.

"Sure you did," Bella countered, congratulating herself silently on keeping her voice so steady. "Here to back out of our dinner date?" she asked with a little too much hope.

His grin broadened and, thankfully, Bella was close enough to the counter that she could hold on and keep her knees from buckling.

"Now why would I do that just when I'm set to get you where I want you so badly?" he asked.

Oh, boy. She really was in way over her head.

"No," he continued when she didn't speak. "I just came to tell you that I'll pick you up at seven, if that's okay."

"Oh, you don't have to," she said. "I can meet you wherever."

"On our first official date?" he countered. "I don't think so. I'll pick you up at your place."

"Fine," she said grudgingly, knowing this was one battle she wasn't going to win. "I'll write down my address."

"Oh, I know where you live."

"What? How?" Oh, she thought. The rental agreement.

"I made it a point to find out," he told her, then leaned across the counter, planted a quick, hard kiss on her open mouth and then winked at her. "So. See you at seven."

"Right. Seven."

"Excellent!" He slapped both hands against the glass counter then beat out a quick, drumlike tattoo of sound with his fingertips. "See you then."

Bella was pretty sure she heard one of her customers give a little sigh. Or, she thought sadly, it might have been her.

Then he turned, directed a brilliant smile at the customers still watching him, lifted a hand in farewell and said, "Ladies…"

The hushed whispers started almost the instant the door swung closed behind him. Bella didn't listen. Instead, she buried herself in work and tried not to think about the coming night.

Jesse left Bella's shop, walked down Main Street and turned left onto Pacific Coast Highway. A small café stood on the corner, with several tiny, round chrome tables clustered together on the sidewalk. There was a great view of the beach, the pier and the men hanging a wide sign reading *Surfing Exhibition—Come See the Champions.*

An exhibition had been his idea. Get a few of his friends together, have some fun in the ocean and rack up some great PR for his company all in one stroke. They'd bring plenty of tourists into town for the day, lots of money would be spent in the shops and he'd get another chance at the limelight. He hated to admit it, but he sort of missed the competition. The excitement of a meet. He didn't miss the press or the photographers, though the exhilaration of a win couldn't be beaten.

Smiling to himself, Jesse took a seat at one of the tables, drummed his fingertips on the shining silver tabletop and waited. When a young blond woman wearing shorts and a red shirt with *Christie's Café* emblazoned across her chest arrived, Jesse said, "Just a coffee, please."

"Sure, Mr. King," the girl said eagerly. "Hey, you're surfing in the exhibition, aren't you?"

"Yeah, I am," he told her, though his thoughts had moved on from the exhibition itself to the woman he thought might be there on the beach watching him.

"That's so great. Can't wait to see you in action!" She swung her long, blond ponytail behind her back and pushed out her breasts, just in case he hadn't noticed them.

Jesse nodded indifferently. He had. He just wasn't interested. Not so long ago, he'd have been smiling back at her, flirting, taking advantage of the gleam in her eyes. Now the only woman he was interested in had more of battle glint in her eyes than a gleam. And that, weirdly enough, was more of a draw for him than the eager blonde.

The waitress grinned hopefully, then disappeared into the café. Jesse was alone, except for the few stragglers taking up spots at the tables. He caught an interested glance cast his way a few times, but he ignored them. One downside to celebrity, he thought—you were never really alone.

"So," a deep voice said from behind him. "Thought we should talk."

Jesse turned his head and watched Bella's friend Kevin walk around him to take a seat in the chair opposite. Before he had a chance to speak, the waitress was back with Jesse's coffee.

"Hi, Kevin," she said. "The usual?"

"Yeah, Tiff. That'd be great." Kevin answered, though his gaze was locked on Jesse.

When she was gone again, Jesse measured the man opposite him. He had the look of a guard dog, which made Jesse wonder just what kind of friendship Kevin and Bella shared. Were they a couple? He didn't like the sound of that, but it was possible, because Jesse never had believed in men and women being merely "friends." But at the same time, he didn't think Bella was the kind of woman to be with one guy and kissing another. So just where did that leave Mr. Guard Dog? What was his interest here?

Jesse kept his irritation tightly wrapped. "What is it you want to talk about? Come to tell me you got those emerald earrings in?"

"No," Kevin said. "Next week. This is about Bella."

Of course it was. Just as well, though, Jesse told

himself. Best to have a little talk with this guy and get a few things straightened out. He wanted to know just where Kevin stood with Bella. Not that it would make a damn bit of difference to Jesse either way. He wanted Bella and he was going to have her. But it would be good to know just how many guys he was going to have to plow through to get to her.

"Fine. Let's talk," Jesse said congenially. "I'll start. Come to warn me off? Because I'll tell you straight up, it won't work."

Before Kevin could answer, the blonde was back, sliding a mug of coffee with cream in front of him. "Thanks," he muttered.

When neither of the men glanced at her again, the blonde pouted briefly and stomped off.

Finally, Kevin picked up his cup, took a sip and set it back down. "I figure Bella can tell you to take a hike if she wants to. That's not why I'm here."

One problem solved. "All right. Then why?"

"I want to know what's going on with you."

"And that's your business because…"

"Because I care about Bella."

Jesse didn't like how that sounded. He didn't like that Kevin felt he had the right to defend Bella. From *him.* His eyes narrowed, his gut clenched and his back teeth ground together. "You *care.* So, you're here to what? Be her white knight?"

"Does she need one?"

"If she does, it won't be you," Jesse told him.

"That's where you're wrong."

Had to give the guy points. He looked harmless, with his easy smile and casual pose. But there was steel inside him, too, which Jesse could admire even as he glared at him. "Have you slept with her?"

Kevin stared back. "No," he said, his voice low and tight.

"Good." Very good, Jesse thought. Even the idea of another man's hands on Bella was enough to set off an unfamiliar sort of rage inside him. He wasn't willing to question why that was. It was enough that the proprietary sensation was there. "Then if you're not her lover, or her husband or her father, what's this about?"

"I'm her friend. More than that," Kevin told him, cupping his coffee cup between his palms. "We're family."

Jesse studied the other man. "Is that right?"

"It is. She was pretty broken up three years ago when you split."

Jesse frowned, not liking the sound of that. He'd never spent a lot of time in self-examination. Usually the women he spent time with were after only what he was—an enjoyable evening. He knew now that Bella didn't fall into that category. Hell, maybe he'd known it back then, too, instinctively. He just hadn't wanted to acknowledge it.

"You're not going to do that to her again," Kevin told him.

"I don't usually take orders."

"Consider it a suggestion."

"Don't like them, either." Jesse braced his elbows on the table and watched Kevin carefully. There was no temper there, no outraged, jealous anger. Just concern. Maybe he was simply Bella's friend. And if so, then he couldn't really blame the guy for looking out for her. But that was Jesse's job now. If she needed protecting, he'd be doing it. What was between Jesse and Bella was nobody else's business. "I'm not asking your permission for anything."

Surprisingly, Kevin laughed. "Oh, hell, no. Man, Bella would kill me if she even knew I was talking to you."

Jesse smiled, but there wasn't much humor in the expression. "So why are you?"

He stood up, laid some money beneath his coffee cup and said, "Bella's not like the kind of woman you're used to. She's real. And she's breakable."

Jesse stood up, too, and slid a ten-dollar bill beneath his own cup in the same motion. "I'm not trying to break her."

"That's the problem," Kevin said with a shrug. "A guy like you can break a woman without even trying."

He left then and Jesse watched him go. *A guy like you.* What the hell did that mean? Was he so different from other men? He didn't think so. As for Bella—he wasn't looking to break her and damn if he would. Jesse wanted her. So Jesse would have her.

"Oh, for God's sake, stop checking the mirror," Bella muttered to herself even as she looked into the glass and smoothed her hands over her hair. She'd been ready for a half hour and had spent the extra time checking and rechecking her reflection.

"Very helpful," she said to the foolish woman looking back at her. Her hair was fine, loose and wavy, hanging down around her shoulders. She wore a black, floor-length skirt and a red blouse with short sleeves and a scooped neckline. The tops of her breasts showed, which made her a little uncomfortable. She stared at that for a minute and thought seriously about changing her shirt.

After all, it was mostly due to Jesse that she'd stopped wearing tight or revealing clothes three years ago. Was she crazy to stroll into the lion's lair looking like a steak?

"Probably," she answered her own silent question, then hissed out an impatient breath and stalked out of the small bathroom, snapping the light off as she went. That's it. She wasn't going to spend one more minute worrying about what she was wearing or how she looked. Despite what Jesse had said in the store that afternoon, this wasn't a *date*. This was dinner. And a bet she had no intention of losing.

When the doorbell rang, she jumped, startled, then grumbling under her breath, headed for the front door. It didn't take long. Her house was small. An old beach cottage, with one bedroom, a tiny bathroom, a serviceable kitchen and a living room only big enough to hold her worktable, a love-seat-size couch and one chair. There were built-in bookcases, though, and room for a TV and stereo. It was small, but it was hers and she loved it, since it was the first real home she'd ever had.

She glanced around, making sure everything was tidy before she opened the door. Jesse stood on her small front porch lined with terra-cotta pots bursting with petunias, pansies and marigolds. The spicy scent of the flowers filled the sultry night air and rushed into her lungs as she inhaled sharply with her first sight of him.

He looked…edible.

His dark blond hair was a little long, hanging over the collar of his white, long-sleeved dress shirt. The collar was open, displaying just a bit of his tanned chest. He wore black slacks, black shoes and a smile that was designed to tempt angels out of heaven.

"You look nice," he said, his gaze resting just a little bit longer than necessary on her breasts. "Are you ready?"

Bella's stomach swirled with nerves that she tried to believe would fade away. But one look into Jesse's eyes assured her that the nervous feeling in her stomach was only going to get worse. All she had to do, she told herself, was to stay strong. *Sure,* she thought as his gaze locked on hers, *no problem.*

"Probably not," she admitted with a shrug, "but let's go anyway."

He laughed softly. "That's the spirit!"

Bella had to smile despite the butterflies still swarming in her stomach. Then she turned, picked up her purse and keys and stepped onto the porch beside him. He closed the door behind her, took her hand in his and said softly, "I've been waiting three years for tonight."

Jesse's house was, naturally, gorgeous. Bella knew it would be from the moment he steered his sports car up a winding driveway to a house that seemed to be perched on top of a hill. It was.

It was also the first shock of the evening.

"It's a 'green' house?" she asked, as they walked toward the front door.

"Right down to the bamboo floors and the recycled glass windows," he told her, grinning at the stunned bemusement on her face. "The builders use concrete. Good insulation, less steel needed for reinforcement and the foundations are easier to lay with less of an impact on the land and—" He broke off, staring at her. "What?"

Bella shook her head. She simply couldn't believe this. He was…more green than she was.

The house was designed to look like an old adobe Spanish-style home. It was surrounded by flowering bushes and dozens of trees. There were solar panels on the roof and wide windows overlooked the ocean, and even the front door looked…rustic.

"I don't believe this," she whispered.

He grinned even more widely. "Surprised? Maybe even…shocked?"

She snapped her head up and stared at him. He'd tricked her neatly because he had to know she never would have believed that he was so environmentally conscious. Why, he was the destroyer and pillager of historic districts. He was the man who was personally turning her beloved hometown into a cookie-cutter community.

And he had jute welcome mats.

Oh God.

She was really in trouble now.

"You set me up, didn't you?"

"You set yourself up, Bella," he said, laughing as he opened the door and ushered her inside. "You assumed you knew everything about me and you were willing to bet on it."

"But you let me," she countered, sweeping past him into the house. Just as she'd thought. It was even more perfect inside than out. Dammit.

"Hell, yes, I let you," he said, chuckling low in his throat so that it sounded like a rumbling freight train.

"You cheated. You knew I'd never expect something like this," she waved both hands out, encompassing the entire house. "I mean, I try to do things the 'green' way, but this is..."

"Why are you so surprised?"

"Are you kidding?" she demanded, glaring at him. "You're the guy who ripped out the heart of the business district and gave it all the personality of a damp rock."

He frowned at her. "That's business. And, just so you know, the materials used were all 'green.'"

"Why? Why do you care?"

"I'm a surfer, Bella. Of course I'm interested in the environment. I want clean oceans and air, I just don't broadcast what I do."

"No, you hide it."

"No, I don't. If you'd bothered to look a little deeper at me, you'd have found plenty of information. The 'Save the Waves' foundation? Mine. King Beach supports it."

She needed to sit down. Bella stared at him, amazed and…impressed. How was she supposed to reconcile her image of the corporate raider with this very unexpected side of Jesse King? Was it possible she'd been wrong about him? And if she were, what else had she been mistaken about?

Her gaze swept the interior. Bamboo floors, shining under coats of polish. Skylights cut into the ceiling allowed moonlight to drift into the foyer, giving the whole house a magical look. And it was working on Bella. She was beyond shocked. She was pleased. And almost proud. How ridiculous was that?

He tucked her hand through his elbow and led her down a long, wide hallway. "Come on. I asked the housekeeper to serve dinner on the patio."

On either side of them, the whitewashed walls were studded with family photos. Her heels tapped against the bamboo floor as she walked beside Jesse. She glanced at the photos as they passed, trying to take them all in. But there were just too many of them.

"Told you I had a lot more at home," he said. "I'll introduce you to all of them after dinner if you want."

Dinner. And, she thought, since he'd managed to absolutely shock her, *she* would be dessert. Unless she backed out. Ran away. Told him she'd changed her mind. He wouldn't be happy about it, but she had no doubt he'd let her leave. He might be arrogant and pushy, but he wasn't a bully.

"You're thinking too much," he said.

"You've given me a lot to think about."

"I knew you'd be shocked, but I still can't help wondering why," he said, leading her through a set of French doors onto a flagstone patio, Bella's breath caught in her throat.

A full moon was up and shining down on the ocean, laying a wide, silver ribbon of a path that looked as though all you had to do was follow it to find something wonderful. Stars winked out of a black sky and a sea wind slid over her skin like a caress. A small, round table was set with white linen, fine china and crystal. A bottle of wine stood open and "breathing" in the center of the table, and candle flames flickered wildly in the protective circle of hurricane-glass globes.

"Wow," she murmured.

"I agree."

She looked at him, but he wasn't looking at the view, or the setting. He was watching *her.* Was it part of his game? His routine for charming women? Or was this something else? Something just for her?

Oh, that thought was certainly a dangerous one.

"This is beautiful," she said, impressed in spite of her own misgivings about being there.

"It really is," he said, moving to the table, and pouring them each a glass of dark red wine. "I found this place the last time I was in Morgan. The setting was great, but I wanted a more organic kind of home. So I rehabbed it." He sent her a quick wink.

"Rehabbing seems to be a hobby of yours."

"Can't help myself. I'm a hands-on kind of guy."

Her stomach swirled and dipped again. Then she

recalled what he'd just said. "You bought this house three years ago?"

"Yeah." He walked toward her, holding out one of the glasses.

She accepted it, took a sip and said, "So you were always planning on moving here."

"Not always," he said. "Actually, it was meeting a certain woman on a pier one night that decided it for me."

He was just too smooth for her. He knew all the right words. Knew all the right moves. And she was floundering. If she had the slightest shred of sense, Bella knew she'd be running from him just as fast as her feet could take her. But she really didn't want to.

"Why do you do things like that?" she asked, her voice little more than a hush.

"Like what?" He sipped at his wine.

"Talk to me as if you're trying to seduce me."

"I am," he said. "I haven't exactly kept it a secret."

"But why play the game?" she asked, walking past him to set her wineglass on the table. With her back to him, Bella said softly, "You don't have to flatter me. Or flirt. Or any of the other things you do to get women. You already know I want you, too. So why bother pretending that you feel something for me that you don't?"

His features went still and, in the moonlight, his blue eyes glittered like silver. His jaw was tight, his hair rippled in the wind. "Who says I don't mean it?"

Eight

Bella turned to look at him and when her gaze locked with his, everything in her sizzled quietly. His eyes looked wild and flashed with heat and desire and something she couldn't quite identify. But whatever it was, there was an answering emotion roiling through her.

"What do you want from me, Jesse?"

He walked toward her, set his glass down beside hers and laid both hands on her shoulders. "Tonight, I just want you. And I don't want it to be because I won the stupid bet." He slid his hands up her shoulders, her neck, to cup her face between his palms. "I want you to come to my bed because you *want* to be there. Because we both *need* to be there."

Bella realized that he was giving her the chance to

back out. But she wouldn't. She'd known the minute Jesse had come back to Morgan Beach that they were headed down this road. That eventually, they would wind up together again. If only for one more night. And if it was going to be only one night, then she was determined to make the most of it.

She wasn't going to hide from what she was feeling anymore. She wasn't going to pretend to hate him. She wasn't going to lie to herself any longer. The simple truth was that she'd fallen in love with him on that night three years ago, when they'd talked about their pasts, their futures, and shared an amazing blaze of passion in the moonlight.

She hadn't wanted to love him. Hadn't expected to. Had tried for three years to hide from the truth behind a curtain of venom because she'd known it couldn't go anywhere. Men like Jesse King didn't settle down. And if they did, they didn't marry women like Bella. So it had been easier to tell herself that she hated him, rather than face the fact that she loved a man she would never have.

But she was done with that now. She did love him, though she'd never tell him that. And she was going to have another night with him—even if that was all she ever got.

She reached up, wrapped her arms around his neck and went up on her toes. "I want to be here, Jesse. With you."

"Thank God," he whispered as he bent his head to take her mouth with his.

Bella's mind splintered as he parted her lips with his tongue and swept inside, stealing what little breath she had left and sharing his own. His tongue stroked hers, tangling them together in a prelude to a dance she'd spent three years hungering for. Her hands splayed against his broad back, holding him to her, as she gave him everything she had and took everything he offered.

His arms tightened around her body, pressing her to him, aligning her body along his with a need so fierce that it inflamed her own. Jesse lifted her easily, swung her up into his arms and Bella felt like a heroine in a romantic movie. Dazed, she lolled against him as he stalked across the patio, through the house and up a set of stairs. She paid no attention to where he was taking her and didn't care, as long as he started kissing her again really soon.

When he finally stopped and set her on her feet again, Bella took a quick look around. They were in his bedroom, obviously. A huge, bamboo four-poster bed took up most of the space. A skylight directly over the bed fanned moonlight onto a black-and-white quilt that looked handmade and what had to be a dozen pillows piled against the intricately carved headboard. Windows provided a view of the moon-kissed ocean and allowed the soft, cool sea wind to glide into the room.

"Like it?" he asked, reading her expression correctly.

"Oh, yes," she said, turning to look up at him.

"You'll like this, too," he told her, stepping past her to flip the quilt back, exposing clean white sheets. "Recycled cotton."

She sighed. "I think I just had an orgasm."

He laughed. "Not yet, baby. But soon. I promise."

Bella looked up at him. "And Kings always keep their promises?"

"Damn straight." He came to her then, hauling her up against him with a hard embrace that sent shivers of excitement scuttling down her spine.

She felt every hard inch of him and her body instantly went into eager mode. She forgot about everything else. Her business, her feud with him, everything. Bella didn't want to think. She wanted to feel.

And Jesse more than obliged.

His kiss turned hot and hungry and frantic. It was as if he couldn't taste her enough and she was right there with him. Her hands slid up and down his back, feeling the pull and flex of lean muscles honed by years of swimming in an ocean that he loved. His arms were like bands of steel, wrapped around her, holding her tightly to him. And when he cupped her bottom and pulled her in even closer, she felt the unmistakable hard length of him pushing into her.

Her body lit up inside and went hot and wet and ready for him. He seemed to sense what she was feeling because he took the hem of her shirt in his big hands and quickly peeled it up and over her head. In seconds, her skirt was gone, too, and she was standing in front of him in her white lace bra and panties.

His hands skimmed up and down her body, following her curves, cupping her breasts until she felt the heat of his touch through the fragile fabric. "Jesse…"

"Don't rush me," he said with a half smile. "I've been waiting a long time for this opportunity."

"No rush," she said and swayed a little unsteadily. "But I think my knees are melting."

That smile kicked up an extra notch. "Let's see what we can do about that."

He led her to the bed, and gave her a gentle push that sent her tumbling onto the mattress. The sheets were cool and smooth beneath her, and Jesse's hands were hard and hot as he continued to explore her. Bella's eyes slid shut on the sensations rippling through her body—there was too much sensory input. Too many feelings. Too many things rushing through her mind, vying for recognition. She was here, in Jesse's bed, with his big hands sliding over her skin, and she knew that no matter what else happened between them, nothing would take away the perfection of this night.

She opened her eyes when he stepped back from her and watched him as he quickly stripped out of his clothes. Through the skylight, a swath of moonlight fell across his naked body and Bella couldn't help thinking how beautiful he was. She smiled and he answered it.

"I remember," he said softly, "just how beautiful you are in moonlight."

"Funny," she answered, "I was just thinking the same thing about you."

One corner of his mouth lifted. "Men aren't beautiful, Bella."

"You are," she assured him and watched new hunger flash in his eyes.

"Enough talk," he told her and leaned over her on the

bed. In a few short seconds, he had her bra undone and off and was sliding her silky panties down her legs to fall to the floor. She twisted beneath him, trying to press herself even more tightly to him, to feel every inch of his hard, warm body along hers.

His hands seemed to be everywhere at once, she thought wildly as passion spiked and desire boiled. Her breasts, her belly, and lower still to the heart of her. Talented fingers and thumb stroked her center, making her writhe beneath him as need built into a firestorm that threatened to engulf her.

Again and again, he pushed her close to the edge of oblivion, only to ease back and keep her from reaching the peak of satisfaction that he held just out of reach. Her hips lifted into his hand as he lowered his head and took first one nipple and then the next into the heat of his mouth. His lips and tongue and teeth scraped and suckled at already too sensitized flesh and Bella was moaning now, from deep in her throat.

Her short, neat fingernails scraped at his back as she twisted beneath him. She slid her hands up, into his thick, golden hair and held him to her as his mouth continued to work at her breasts. "Jesse…"

"Soon," he promised, his words a whisper of a caress against her flesh.

It had to be soon, or she would die of the wanting. She felt her body coiling tighter and tighter and knew she couldn't take much more of his. "I need you. Inside. Jesse, please."

He lifted his head, stared down at her and she saw

the same passion she was feeling mirrored in his eyes. Her heart turned over in her chest and something wild and wonderful spilled through her bloodstream. There was more here than want. More than just need. There was a soul-deep connection between them. She felt it. Knew it. Recognized it.

Then he kissed her, plunging his tongue deeply into her mouth and thoughts scattered like dead leaves in a cold wind. His fingers continued to stroke and tease her, even as he moved to settle himself between her thighs.

She lifted her hips in silent invitation and when he eased back from their kiss, sitting on his haunches to look down at her, Bella felt like the most beautiful woman on the face of the planet. He looked at her with such a craving, she felt powerful and strong and enticing.

He parted her thighs farther, sliding his hands up and down the inside of her legs until she hissed in a breath and whispered brokenly, "Jesse, now."

"Yeah," he agreed, pushing his body into hers in one long, heated slide, "*now.*"

She groaned as he filled her and her body stretched to accommodate him. He held perfectly still inside her for one long moment. Until she moved beneath him, showing him that she was ready for him. For all he could give her.

Jesse watched her eyes glaze and felt the thrumming of her heartbeat as he lowered his head to kiss her breasts, each in turn. His own heartbeat was galloping in his chest. He couldn't seem to catch his breath and he didn't care. This was what he'd been searching for these last three years. This woman. This moment. This link.

But as she sinuously moved beneath him, his mind blanked and his body took over. There would be time for thinking later. Much later. For now, he had everything he could want, right here in his arms.

He moved within her—sure, long strokes designed to draw the pleasure out, to stoke it so high they might both burn in the aftermath. Again and again, he laid claim to her and with every stroke. She met him, lifting her hips into him, sliding into a smooth rhythm he'd found with no one else. It was as if their bodies recognized what their minds had been fighting. That they belonged together. They *fit.*

He braced his hands on either side of her head, looked down into chocolate-brown eyes that sparkled and shone in the moonlight and gave himself up to what was happening. He felt her body stiffen, knew the moment when her climax claimed her and watched the magic in her eyes. Only then did he allow himself to follow after, his body shattering.

When the last of the tremors finally ceased, he collapsed atop her and felt her arms come around him, cradling him to her chest.

The night passed too quickly and Jesse couldn't seem to get enough of her. Again and again, they made love and each time was better than the one before. They came together, dozed briefly, then made love again. Finally, around 2:00 a.m., they threw on robes and raided the kitchen, at last getting around to eating the meal his housekeeper had left for them. It was cold, but they didn't care. They drank wine, ate their meal and then he had her as dessert on the kitchen table.

He couldn't keep his hands off her and even as he experienced it, Jesse knew how different this was for him. He'd never wanted a woman to stay the night with him before. And with Bella, he didn't want her to leave. As long as he kept her there, at his house, nothing would change.

Once the world intruded, everything would be different.

But he couldn't ignore the dawn. Jesse was used to waking up early. The habit came from all those years of pulling on a wet suit and heading to the beach to sit on a board and watch the rising sun blaze across the surface of the water. As far as he was concerned, the dawn was still the best part of the day.

Bella was sleeping when he slipped out of bed to start a pot of coffee. His housekeeper wouldn't arrive until noon, so breakfast would be up to him. He smiled as he thought about taking Bella some coffee and then convincing her to take a nice, hot shower with him.

Still smiling, he hit the button on the coffeepot, then walked through the quiet house to the front door. He stepped outside, picked up the paper off the porch, then went back into the house, unfolding the paper as he strolled at a leisurely pace back to the kitchen.

While he waited for the pot to brew, he leaned back against the counter and flipped through the thin, local paper, checking out the news and admiring the ad King

Beach was running. He finally hit the editorial page and paused to pour his first cup of the day. Taking a sip, he skimmed the letters to the editor and smiled as he read the complaints on everything from skateboarding kids to dogs being unwelcome on the beach.

"Gotta love a small town," he murmured, "there's always someone with something to say—"

Then he spotted one specific letter and scowled. He shot a glance at the floor above him, then deliberately took a breath, poured two more cups of coffee and tucking the paper under his arm, headed for the master bedroom. Bella was still snuggled under the quilt when he walked in and just for a second, he thought about ignoring the stupid newspaper in favor of joining her on the big bed.

Then he shook his head, and crossed the room. Sitting on the edge of the mattress, he set the coffee on the side table and reached down to smooth her hair back from her face. She was beautiful. And terribly sneaky.

"Bella," he said, "wake up."

"What? Why?" She pulled the pillow over her head and slipped deeper beneath the quilt.

Jesse plucked the pillow free, tossed it aside and said again, "Come on, wake up."

One brown eye opened and glared at him. "Jesse, it's still *dark.*"

"It's dawn and the paper's here. The Morgan Beach weekly." He was watching her, waiting for her to respond.

"That's nice." She sniffed and blinked blearily at him. "I smell coffee."

"Have some," he said, offering her the cup as she scooted around and pushed a pillow behind her back. The sheet was drawn up, covering her breasts, and her hair was tousled. She looked beautiful. And so damn innocent.

Funny, in all his plans for her, he'd never once considered that she might still be working against him. Plotting. Planning. Turns out, he should have.

She took a sip, sighed, then blinked again, trying to focus on him. "Why are we awake?"

"I always wake up early."

"That's a hideous habit," she said sleepily, giving him a soft smile, "made slightly less hideous by the fact that you at least provide coffee."

"Uh-huh," he said, holding the newspaper up. "And reading material."

"What?" She stared at the paper he'd folded to a specific section. A second or two ticked past before her eyes went wide and she whispered, "Oh, no."

"Oh, yes," he said, both eyebrows rising high on his forehead. "Your letter to the editor was printed this morning."

"Jesse..."

"Wait, I want to read you my favorite part," he said, fixing his gaze on the short, to-the-point letter she'd written.

"Morgan Beach is selling its soul to a corporate raider who doesn't care what happens to us and our homes as long as his company makes a profit. We should all band together and let Jesse King

know that we won't be bought. We won't surrender who we are. Morgan Beach was here before Jesse King and it will be here long after he tires of playing at being a member of this community."

Bella's eyes closed and a groan slipped from her throat. She covered her eyes with one hand as if she couldn't bring herself to look at him. Her expression was one of pure misery and Jesse didn't mind admitting to himself that he was glad about that, at least.

"Very nice," he said, sarcasm icing his tone. "I especially like the 'corporate raider' part. Seems to be a theme with you. And the rest of it's pretty good, too. You should be a writer."

"I was angry."

"Was?" he repeated, picking up on that one word. "So you're not anymore?"

She hitched the sheet a little higher, then scooped one hand through her hair, swiping it back from her face. "I don't know."

"Great, you don't know," he said, standing up and walking to one of the windows. Jesse felt as if he'd been kicked in the gut. He had known all along that Bella had a problem with what he'd been doing since he hit town, but damn.

She'd just spent the night with him, all the time knowing that she'd taken another public shot at him.

Thoughts of the night before rushed through his mind. How could she have been so eager, so responsive, if this is how she still felt about him? Strange, but he felt used. And suddenly, he realized how all the women in his life must have been left feeling.

Hell of a time for an epiphany.

He stared blindly out at the ocean and tried to ignore the rustle of bedsheets that told him she was getting up. But even pissed, his insides twisted, knowing she was close by and naked. How twisted was that, he wondered, to want the one woman who hated his guts?

A moment later, she joined him at the window, his black-and-white quilt wrapped around her curvy body like a toga.

"I'd forgotten all about writing that letter," she said.

"If that's an apology, it sucks." He tossed the newspaper onto a chair and took a gulp of his coffee.

"It's not an apology," she said. "I meant it when I wrote it so I can't apologize for that."

He glanced at her. "Great." He paused, then asked, "Did you mean all that? Do you really think I don't care what happens to this place?"

"Jesse," she said with a shake of her head, "when I moved here, I loved it." She looked out the window at the ocean and the sunrise, just staining the horizon. "I'd never really had a home before. I...grew up in the foster system."

She said it so matter-of-factly, Jesse couldn't even offer sympathy. But he remembered how longingly she'd looked at the photos of his family, how she'd seemed so caught up in the fact that they were a huge, yet close group. And then he thought about what it must have been like to grow up alone. What it might have been like for him if he hadn't had his brothers and cousins. He couldn't help feeling a stab of sympathy for the little girl she'd once been, who'd had nowhere to call home.

And he wondered a bit that he could feel so much for her. He should have stayed pissed. Yet…looking at her, he just couldn't seem to hold on to the feeling.

"I loved the funky little buildings on Main Street," she was saying, "the slow pace of town life, the cottages on the beach. The sense of community. I saw it and knew that I belonged here, as if I'd never belonged anywhere before. I spent the first year here sliding into the town, making my place, fitting in." She turned her head and looked up at him. "You moved in and immediately started changing everything."

Frowning, Jesse thought he could understand now just why she'd been fighting him so hard for so long. "Nothing ever stays the same."

"I suppose not," she said wistfully and turned her head again to watch the sunrise splashing brilliant color across the ocean.

"So, change is bad, is that it?"

"Not bad, it's just *change,*" she argued. "I don't like it. I love this town. I loved what it was and I was angry at you for—"

"Buying up its soul?" he quoted, feeling the sting of the words again. He'd never meant to be a corporate raider. Hadn't wanted to be a corporate *anything.* And yet, somehow it had happened to him. He'd made his peace with it. Even come to enjoy what he'd made of his life. Until he found Bella. And now suddenly, he was left feeling that, somehow, the success he'd achieved was only failure, cleverly disguised.

She closed her eyes. "I'm sorry. I didn't mean to hurt you—well, no, I guess I did mean to. But that was before."

"Before you were back in my bed?" he asked, feeling a small stab of temper. "Guess it would be a little embarrassing to be attacking in public the same guy you're sleeping with in private."

"It's not that, Jesse," she said, clutching her toga to her chest tightly with one hand. "I think I might have been wrong about you and—"

"Might? *Might* have been wrong?" He laughed shortly. "Well, hell, Bella. That's damn nice of you."

With her free hand, Bella reached out, grabbed his upper arm and held on. Looking up into his eyes, she said, "I was wrong about you. I admit it. I wanted to hate you because it was easier that way. I wanted you to leave Morgan Beach because I didn't want to have to see you and not have you. I wanted…"

"What?" he asked, his voice low, his gaze fixed on her.

"You, Jesse," she said. "I wanted *you,* and couldn't admit it, even to myself."

He took a breath, inhaling the fresh, clean scent of her, then reached out and skimmed his fingers through her thick, soft hair. His gaze moved over her, settled on her mouth briefly and then lifted to meet her troubled eyes. "And now you're admitting it?"

She deliberately released her hold on the quilt and it swished to the floor at her feet. Moving into him, she slid her hands up over his chest and then hooked her arms behind his neck. "I'm admitting it. I'll even write a retraction to the paper, if you want."

He gave her a lazy smile, dismissing the irritation of seeing her letter in the paper in favor of enjoying having her in his arms. "I think I prefer a more private apology."

"Oh, I'm not apologizing," she corrected, going up on her toes to kiss him once, twice. "I'm just saying that I'm revising my opinion."

"Enough to consider making Bella's Beachwear a part of King Beach?" he asked.

She huffed out a breath. "Enough to think about considering it."

He laughed a little. "I can live with that."

Then he picked her up, carried her to the bed and lost himself once again in the wonder of her.

Nine

Everything was different, Bella thought.

Since that incredible night with Jesse a few days ago, they'd been together nearly every day. She was at King Beach or he was at her shop and they were talking business. He'd asked her advice on how to make his swimwear "greener" and had actually listened to her opinions. He was meeting her weavers and seamstresses and still trying to talk her into joining King Beach.

And for the first time, Bella was tempted. She still wasn't interested in success just for the sake of making money. But he'd dangled the hope of reaching women nationwide with her specialty suits and that was something she couldn't easily dismiss. With King Beach, she could find ways to make her cottage industry viable in a bigger sctting and still maintain the kind of quality she insisted on.

But more than all that, being with Jesse was becoming the best part of her days. And nights. They were together every night now. At his house. At her house. On the beach, recapturing their very first time together. Her heart was full. She felt…amazing.

And she was terrified.

Bella was in love and just knew it wasn't going to end well. Despite how attentive he was now, Jesse King was simply not the forever kind of guy. Sooner or later, he'd get tired of what they had and he'd move on. And Bella knew the pain that was headed her way was something she might never recover from.

In self-defense, she should have started pulling away from him. Keeping a safe distance between her heart and Jesse. But she couldn't bring herself to give up what she could have now to protect herself in the future. Wasn't it better to enjoy what you had while you had it? There would always be time for pain later.

"You're thinking about him again."

She blinked, looked at Kevin and smiled. "How can you tell?"

"You're drooling."

Quickly, she lifted one hand to her mouth, then sneered at her best friend. "Oh, that's very funny."

He smiled at her over the lunch table. "You look happy, Bella. It's nice to see."

"I am happy," she said, but her voice carried a wary tone.

"But..."

"But," she said, stirring her iced tea, "it's not going to last, Kevin. One of these days, Jesse's going to move on and I'm not looking forward to it."

"How do you know?" He reached across the table and patted her hand. "Seems to me he's spending a lot of time with you. A guy doesn't do that if he's not interested."

"I know," she said, and pushed her plate aside. She wasn't really hungry anyway. "He's interested now. But how long can it last?"

"Jeez, Bella." Kevin shook his head at her. "Maybe you should give him a chance to screw up before you punish him."

"I'm not punishing him," she argued.

"Maybe not, but you're already rehearsing your goodbye speech."

"I'm just preparing myself," she countered, "and you'd think that my best friend would approve."

"Your best friend thinks you're nuts," Kevin told her, sitting back in his chair and crossing his arms over his chest. "Seriously, when you don't have him, you're miserable. When you *do* have him, you're crazy. Women are nuts."

"Thanks. Have you told Traci your theory?" His girlfriend, a model for one of the bigger agencies in California, was constantly traveling and had been gone from Morgan Beach for almost four weeks this time.

"Of course," he said. "She says I'm wrong. Just like you. But you're women. You can't see it."

"Uh-huh, and if we're crazy, why do you guys want to be with us?"

He grinned. "So where's Mr. Wonderful today anyway? You haven't had lunch with me in more than a week. Usually you're with him."

"He said he had to meet someone. Didn't say who." Bella frowned a little.

"So naturally, you're thinking it's some other woman."

Bella's eyes widened. "Well, I wasn't. Until now."

Kevin sighed. "Eat your alfalfa sprouts."

"She's making me insane," Jesse muttered.

"Not so hard to do if you ask me," Justice King told his younger brother and affixed his pliers to the end of the barbed wire before twisting it around a fence post.

"That's nice, thanks." Jesse shoved his hands into his jeans pockets and stared out over the rolling hills and fields of his brother's ranch. There was a cold wind blowing and afternoon sunshine spilled out of a sky studded with massive gray clouds. Idly, Jesse wondered if they might be in for an end-of-summer storm.

He'd made the two-hour trip to Justice's ranch in just under an hour and a half. He'd picked up a speeding ticket along the way, but it had still been worth it. He'd needed to get out of Morgan Beach. Needed a little distance from Bella. Needed to clear his head and driving fast was one sure way to do it.

He was seeing way too much of her, he told himself. Every day. Every night. She was becoming a part of him, threading herself so seamlessly into his life, he couldn't even imagine a way of getting her out again. When he was with her, he was touching her. When he wasn't with her, he was thinking about her.

What the *hell* was happening to his life?

"This is serious, Justice," he said, shooting a glare at his older brother. "She's slipping into my life and I'm letting it happen."

"Maybe that's a good thing," Justice told him, snipping off the end of the wire and tucking it into his jeans pocket. "Maybe you're tired of the babe-of-the-week routine. Ready for something different. Permanent."

His insides went cold and still. "Hold on, nobody said anything about permanent."

"Crap, you just went white." Justice laughed, walked back to his truck and set the pliers down in the locked down toolbox in the bed. "It's good to see."

"Yeah, because it worked out so well for you."

Instantly, Justice's grin faded. "What happened between me and Maggie has nothing to do with anything."

"Sure, we can talk about me, but not Maggie." Jesse kicked at the dirt, sent a spray of it toward the truck and glared at his brother.

"You came to me, Jesse. Remember?" Justice tugged the brim of his dust-colored cowboy hat down low over his eyes. "If you're having problems with a woman they're *your* problems, not mine."

"Fine. Forget it. Damn close-mouthed bastard." Justice never had told anyone what had gone wrong between him and his estranged wife, Maggie Ryan. The wholc family had been nuts about Maggie, yet one day she and Justice had separated, neither of them offering an explanation.

That was a year ago, and still, his brother was completely mute on the subject.

After a minute or two, Jesse blurted, "Look, you're the only one of us to ever get married. Who the hell else should I ask?"

"Try Travis. Or Jackson. Or hell, even Adam," Justice told him, ticking off the names of three King cousins who'd all been happily married for a couple of years now.

"They're not around—you are."

"Lucky me."

"How the hell is a man supposed to deal with having only one woman in his life?" Jesse asked. "I've never done that before. Never had a long-standing girlfriend. Never wanted one. I like the no-strings-attached approach to dating, you know?"

"So, have no strings," Justice told him.

"But Bella's not that kind of woman," Jesse muttered, shoving one hand through his hair. "She's got strings all over the damn place and I keep getting tangled up in them."

"You don't want them?" Justice said quietly, as he closed the gate on the back of the truck. "Cut them and move on. End of story."

Jesse looked at his brother and sighed. Justice was right, he knew it. And yet, "That's the problem. For the first time in my life, I don't know if I want to move on."

* * *

The surfing exhibition had drawn a great crowd. People from up and down the state had gathered in Morgan Beach to watch the show and so far, it had been worth it.

Some of the best surfers in the world were riding the waves, making it look effortless as they skimmed the surface of the water, riding in a tunnel of water, then shooting out into the open, their boards kicking up fantail wakes behind them. The sun slipped in and out of banks of heavy clouds, its golden light glancing off the surface of the water in nearly blinding flashes. The scent of hot dogs and beer wafted over the noisy crowd and seagulls shrieked in accompaniment. The exhibition was proving to be a great end-of-summer celebration and the crowds would no doubt spill over into the Main Street shops later. But for now, Bella had her shop closed so she could watch the show. And Jesse.

She had a great seat in the bleachers set up in the sand for the day. At the end of a row, she looked down to her left at the path the surfers took in and out of the water. And she wasn't alone, either. Jesse's cousin, Jackson, his wife, Casey, and their daughters, Mia and Molly, were in town. They'd actually come to southern California to take the girls to Disneyland, but hadn't been able to resist watching Jesse surf in the competition.

"He's really good, isn't he?" Casey whispered, her gaze locked on the ocean where Jesse was maneuvering his long board in and out of a six-foot wave.

Cheers erupted from the stands and Bella grinned,

caught up in the excitement of watching Jesse do what he did best. He had so much grace and style, he eclipsed every other surfer out there easily. And everyone in the stands seemed to recognize that, too.

"He really is good," Bella answered, never taking her eyes off the man who'd become such a huge part of her life. She couldn't even believe how charmed her life was lately. Every spare moment was spent with Jesse and she grew more in love with him every day. The only worry was that she didn't know how he felt.

Did he share her feelings? Or was this all just a fun fling that he'd move on from eventually? And if it was, how would she ever get through it?

She closed her eyes, sighed and told herself not to worry about that now. Just to enjoy this moment for what it was. She was building so many memories, her heart was full of them.

"Of course he is," Jackson said, "he's a King, isn't he? Molly, honey, don't eat the paper."

"Paper?" Casey demanded, tearing her gaze from the ocean to look at her younger daughter. "What paper?"

"Nothing, don't worry about it," Jackson told her. "Let's just consider it fiber."

Bella laughed, Casey sighed and reached across her husband to lift her two-year-old daughter onto her lap. "Honestly, Jackson."

"I didn't tell her to eat the paper the cookie came in, did I, Mia?" He tickled his older daughter and as the girl laughed, Bella sighed.

Jesse's cousin and his family had arrived in town the night before and since then, they'd all had a wonderful time together. Jesse was like a different person when he was with the two little girls. They clearly adored him and he was crazy about them. Watching him with Jackson's daughters, Bella hadn't been able to stop the tiny bubble of something dangerously maternal rising inside her. And she wondered what it would be like to be Jesse's wife. To have his children. To feel that sort of warmth surrounding her for the rest of her life.

But the truth was, as much as she loved him, as much as she wanted him, Bella wasn't sure he felt the same way. Yes, he was a wonderful lover. But did it go any further than that? Was she in love and he in lust? She wished she knew.

"Where's Uncle Jesse?" Mia demanded, standing on her father's lap and staring out at the sea.

"There he is," Bella said and pointed to the surfer sitting atop his board, waiting for his next ride. "See? When the next wave comes, he'll stand up and ride it all the way in to the beach."

"Can I?" Mia asked.

"Sure," Jackson told her. "When you're thirty."

Casey caught Bella's eye and winked. "He's a little overprotective."

"I think it's nice," Bella said.

"Me, too, actually," Casey admitted. "He and his brothers guard their kids like trained pit bulls. It's really amazing to watch. And when the kids are all together, it's hysterical, seeing all the King boys riding herd on them."

"It's not funny," Jackson told her, "it's stressful."

"I think it sounds wonderful." Bella smiled, but Casey looked at her with sympathy.

Leaning in closely, she whispered, "Falling for a King isn't easy, Bella. They'll make you nuts if you let them. But I promise, it's completely worth it."

She nodded, but couldn't help thinking that it would be worth it if the King you loved, loved you back. Otherwise, it was just torture.

"There he goes!" Mia shouted, jumping up and down on her daddy's lap and pointing excitedly at Jesse.

Bella stilled her thoughts and focused on his last ride of the day. It was perfect. Jesse lay across his board and paddled fiercely until the crest of the rising wave caught up to him. Then he stood, shook back his hair and walked up and down the length of the board with an easy grace that was beautiful to watch. His arms were relaxed at his sides and even from a distance, Bella could see his grin while he used his body to direct the board in and out of the wave. The roar of the ocean was lost in the roar of the crowd's appreciation. His ride ended as his board skimmed the lacy froth of the dying wave. He jumped off as he neared the shore, then picked up the board, tucked it under his arm and trotted up the beach.

Bella watched as literally hundreds of bikini-clad women raced toward him, all of them eagerly attempting to capture his attention. He ran past them all as if he didn't even see them. Bella's breath caught as he headed right toward her. Her heart pounded hard in her chest as he dropped his board to the sand, looked up at her and asked, "How'd I do?"

"Great!" Jackson shouted then grunted when his wife's elbow met his midsection. "Hey, what was that for?"

"He wasn't talking to you," Casey muttered.

Jesse grinned wider. "She's right. I wasn't. Bella. How'd I do?"

"You were wonderful," she said, aware now that people all around them were watching, listening.

"That's what I like to hear. Now I need my prize."

Bella laughed. "No trophies today, remember?"

"Who's talking about a trophy?" Jesse asked, and reaching up, plucked her from the bleachers and dragged her down to him. "This is the only reward I'm interested in."

Then he kissed her. Long and hard and deep, sweeping her backward into a romantic dip that had the audience surrounding them cheering in approval.

Vaguely, Bella was aware of the crowd's applause and even of the sound of cameras clicking as pictures were snapped. But she didn't care. How could she when Jesse's arms were around her and his mouth was fused to hers? Electricity hummed through her body and sent sparks shooting through her bloodstream.

He'd sought her out. Come to her. Kissed her in front of the whole world and for the first time in her life, Bella felt like a princess. Like she mattered. Her heart turned over in her chest and she felt even more deeply in love, though she wouldn't have thought that possible.

Finally, after what felt like a lifetime, he broke the kiss, lifted his head to stare into her eyes and Bella thought she saw…love shining back at her.

Then he grinned, the moment was gone and she couldn't be sure it had even happened. Instantly, the crowd surrounded them, congratulating Jesse on his win and he draped one arm around her shoulders, holding her close to his side.

Did he love her?

She didn't know. But the sun was shining and he was holding her tight and just for the moment, that was enough.

Later that night at Bella's house, they sat out on the top step of the back porch, sipping wine and watching the clouds sail past the moon. From Mrs. Clayton's house next door, came the sounds of a game show playing on TV and from down the street came the howl of a dog. On the other side of Bella's place, Kevin's house was dark.

The spicy scent of chrysanthemums planted along the back fence filled the air, and Jesse took a deep breath, drawing it deep, knowing that he would always associate that scent with this night. With this woman.

He draped one arm around her and smiled when she leaned into him, laying her head on his shoulder. "It was a good day."

"It was," she agreed, taking a sip of wine. "You were amazing out on the water."

"Not bad for a corporate raider, huh?" he asked, his tone light and teasing.

She huffed out a breath. "Not going to let me forget that anytime soon, are you?"

"No, I figure that's good for at least six months' worth of teasing."

"Six months?"

"At least," he said, looking down into those chocolate eyes of hers.

"So you think we'll still be together," she said, "like this, I mean, in six months?"

He frowned and felt her tense up alongside him. "Well, yeah. Why wouldn't we be?"

She tipped her head back and stared up at the moon as clouds drifted across its face. "I just didn't know how you felt. What you expected."

"I don't *expect* anything, Bella," he said, turning on the step to face her more fully. "We're good together, aren't we?"

"Yes."

"The sex is great."

"Yes," she said, smiling.

"Well, then." That was settled. It was like he'd told Justice, he didn't want to move on. He liked being with Bella. He liked who he *was* with Bella. But he felt hesitation in her and he knew that she was thinking again. Trying to lay out a plan. Or see into the future. "Why should we try to put a time stamp on this? Or define it somehow? Look, nobody knows what's going to happen to them a day from now, let alone six months from now. But here, tonight, I can't imagine being anywhere else."

It was the closest he'd ever come to telling a woman that he didn't want to lose her.

She looked at him for a long moment, then smiled and laid one hand on his forearm. "Me, either."

Jesse smiled. Problem averted. For now, anyway.

She changed the subject abruptly though and he had to wonder if she did it on purpose, trying to keep him off balance. If so, she was damn good at it.

"I liked your cousin and his family."

His smile broadened. "Yeah. Always good to see them and the kids."

"I envy you that," she whispered.

"What?" He kissed the top of her head, silently encouraging her to continue.

"Your family. You're all so connected. And you were so good with those little girls..."

He dismissed that easily. "They're great kids. Not hard to have fun with them."

"Yes," she said, tipping her head back to look up at him, "but a lot of men wouldn't bother to get down on the floor and give 'pony rides' for an hour."

He laughed, but she only looked at him, so his laughter faded away quickly. "What is it?"

"I've been doing a lot of thinking lately."

"Okay..." Her expression was serious. Damn near solemn, and Jesse braced himself for whatever might be coming.

"And I've come to the conclusion that you aren't quite the man I thought you were in the beginning."

He smiled at her. "Good to know."

She straightened up and looked him square in the eye. "There's more. Jesse, you know I never wanted to expand my business."

"Yeah," he said wryly, relaxing just a bit. "I think you've made that pretty clear."

"Well, I've changed my mind."

"What?" That surprised him and he wondered idly if he'd ever be able to read Bella. He watched her, trying to determine her emotions, but her eyes were clear and direct and whatever she was feeling, she kept hidden too well for him to decipher.

Finally, she smiled, lifted her hand and cupped his cheek in her palm. He felt the warmth of her slide deep inside him.

"I've decided to join King Beach," she said. "You've convinced me that I can trust you, Jesse. And I think, together, we can do some amazing things."

He caught her hand in his and squeezed it. Strange, but over the last couple of weeks, he'd forgotten about trying to merge her company into King Beach. He'd been too focused on getting her into bed. And then keeping her there once he had her. Her making this announcement out of the blue really threw him.

He was utterly touched. For weeks, he'd been trying to make her see reason. To join King Beach. Now that she had, he felt a little...uneasy. But why? He'd bought up companies before. Hell, he'd gotten his start that way. But for Bella to join him was a real statement on her part. She was trusting him not to ruin what she loved. "You won't be sorry, Bella."

"I know," she said, leaning into him for a kiss. "I believe in you, Jesse."

The wind kicked up, carrying the scent of the sea, and a trickle of worry sprang up out of nowhere inside him. Promptly, Jesse shut it down. This was what he'd wanted. And hell, he'd done even better than he'd thought. Not only did he have her business, but he had *Bella.*

What could possibly go wrong?

Three days after the exhibition, life was back to normal in Morgan Beach. Except for one thing.

Jesse was nervous.

This was not normal. Not for him anyway.

He was worried about his relationship with Bella now that they would be going into business together. What if she found out that he'd planned to seduce her into handing over the reins? She'd be hurt, pissed. He hadn't expected to care, but he did.

And he couldn't bear the thought of losing her.

But he didn't like hiding the truth from her, either. He'd learned long ago that hidden secrets had a way of showing up when you least expected them to bite you in the ass.

So what did that say? What the hell was he feeling and why now of all times? Bella had sneaked up on him and he'd never seen it coming. She'd gotten beneath his finely tuned radar and had carved out a spot for herself in his heart. Hell, he hadn't even known he could feel everything he was feeling for her. Hadn't guessed he was capable of it.

For years, he'd steered clear of anything that looked like it might lead to something permanent. Carefully, deliberately, he'd only dated women who were interested in having a good time. The future-in-their-eyes type he left strictly alone.

So how the hell had this happened to him?

Which wasn't really important now anyway. The real question was, what was he going to do about it?

For three days now, he'd kept his distance from Bella, trying to work out in his own mind just what he was feeling and what he wanted to do about it. This was a whole new ball game for him. He'd never before even contemplated a future with a woman. He'd never before *wanted* to. Now, he couldn't imagine the rest of his life without Bella beside him.

God knew, he hadn't meant to get so involved. He'd wanted Bella mostly to prove something to Nick Acona. Now it had gone way beyond that. And damn if he knew how to handle it.

He stood up from his desk, turned around and stared out the bank of windows at Main Street and the ocean beyond. Black clouds hovered on the horizon, pushing toward shore and he knew that by evening, there'd be a storm blowing in. Which suited how he was feeling just fine. His insides were raging, in a tumult. He'd never thought of himself as the marrying kind of guy. But Bella was definitely the marriage kind of woman. Which left them exactly where?

His parents' marriage hadn't gone well, what with his father always buried in work. And Justice's marriage had split apart, though no one knew why. So how the hell was he supposed to make it work?

"Mr. King?"

"Yeah?" He glanced over his shoulder, irritated at the interruption as he watched Dave Michaels step into the office. "What is it, Dave?"

Dave blinked at Jesse's tone, but said, "I've got the paperwork drawn up for Bella to look over and sign."

"Right. Fine. Just…leave it on my desk, will you?" He turned back to stare outside again, his thoughts racing in circles. He'd convinced Bella to take a chance. To sign with King Beach. To trust him not to screw up the business she loved.

And he couldn't help feeling guilty about it all. He'd won. This was what he'd set out to do. To seduce her and persuade her to join his company. Everything had gone according to his original plan. He'd submarined her. Coaxed her into sharing the most important thing in her life.

The only trouble was, while he was seducing her, *he* was the one who'd been falling.

He'd stumbled into a snare that only tightened when he tried to escape. But then, he told himself, maybe that was because he didn't really want to get free.

He groaned and shoved one hand through his hair. His life had been a lot less complicated before he'd come to Morgan Beach.

There were two customers in her store, a new order just arriving from the seamstresses and a tidy profit sitting in the bank, thanks to the sales made on the day of the surfing exhibition.

So why wasn't Bella happier?

She frowned as she fitted the new swimwear onto hangers and sorted them by size and style. She knew the answer to that question. Because she hadn't seen Jesse since she'd agreed to join King Beach.

Oh, she'd talked to him on the phone several times. He was busy. Had meetings. Decisions had to be made. Papers drawn up. He said all the right things, and when she was talking to him it all made perfect sense. It was later, when she was alone, that the niggling doubts crept into her mind to torture her.

She missed Jesse, too. Missed his smile. His laugh. The feel of his arms sliding around her. The whisper of his breath against her neck.

But if he was feeling the same things, why was he staying away from her?

Bella shook her head, tried to dismiss her thoughts and smiled at a woman browsing through the racks. She went back to her work, all the time her mind whirling with possibilities, each worse than the one before.

He'd gotten what he wanted, now he didn't need to see her anymore. She shook her head, not liking the sound of that at all.

Romancing her had simply been part of the plan, to wear down her defenses and get hold of her company. That one she liked even less. He couldn't have been pretending, could he? Was anyone that good an actor?

He was feeling guilty for stealing her company under false pretenses, so he couldn't bring himself to face her. Hmph. She didn't think so. Jesse King didn't do guilt.

"So what's going on?" she muttered, her stomach twisting itself into knots.

And why was she standing around wringing her hands about it? For heaven's sake, all she had to do was go to him and tell him she wanted to know what was going on. They were partners now, weren't they? In business *and* in life. If she had questions, then she'd take them straight to Jesse. This might have nothing to do with her, after all. It might be a family problem. Something she could help him with.

Nodding to herself, Bella decided that as soon as these customers left the shop, she'd go to the King Beach office and make Jesse talk to her.

The front door opened, the bell above it jangling, and Bella looked up. A man in a three-piece suit approached the counter. "Bella Cruz?"

"Yes," she said, giving him her best, I'm-the-owner-welcome-to-my-store-smile. "How can I help you?"

He nodded, tucked one hand into the inside pocket of his suit jacket and withdrew an envelope. "I was instructed to deliver this." He handed it over. "Have a nice day."

Then he turned and left. Before the bell had stopped jangling again, Bella had the envelope open and was pulling the folded, single sheet of paper from inside. She read it. Then read it again.

Her insides iced over and a cold, hard knot of pain

settled in the pit of her stomach. The letters on the paper blurred as tears swam in her eyes. Determinedly though, she blinked them back. She wasn't going to cry. She was going to scream. Fury erupted, clawing at her throat, nearly choking her.

This couldn't be right, she thought, her gaze locked on a few, select words. Had to be a mistake. But then, a quiet, logical voice in her mind whispered, it explains a lot, doesn't it? Why Jesse'd been avoiding her, for example. And as her thoughts raced, the sense of betrayal blossomed inside her until she thought she would explode.

She'd wondered what was going on.

Now she knew.

But she couldn't do a thing about it until her customers were gone. With that thought in mind, she plastered on a helpful smile, tucked the paper into the pocket of her skirt and went to work. The sooner she helped these women find what they'd come for, the sooner she could face Jesse King.

If he thought she'd simply disappear, he was sadly mistaken.

He was about to find out exactly what Bella thought of him.

Ten

A knock on his office door had Jesse frowning an hour later. Before he could shout, *come in,* the door opened and Dave Michaels stuck his head inside. He looked worried. Never a good sign.

"Boss, there's a problem."

"What? What problem?"

"Oh," Bella said, pushing past Dave to stomp into the office, "there's more than just a problem."

Dave's expression went from concerned to panicked. Jesse hardly noticed though, because his attention was focused on the absolutely infuriated woman standing in front of his desk. Bella's eyes were flashing like danger signals and her mouth was flattened into a grim slash. She was practically vibrating with rage.

"Thanks, Dave," Jesse said, waving one hand to dismiss the man. "I'll take it from here."

Obviously grateful for the reprieve, Dave backed out and closed the door behind him.

Jesse stood up from his chair, walked around the desk and headed for Bella. Worry raced through him, but he squelched it. He'd fix whatever was wrong.

She backed up, shook her head at him and held out one hand to stave him off. "Don't you even come near me, you bastard."

Surprised, he stared at her. "Now just a minute..."

"It was all a game, wasn't it?" she said, her voice cold, tight, pitched low enough that he had to strain to hear her. She wasn't shouting or shrieking. Trust Bella to be different from every other woman he'd ever known. The few times he'd faced down a furious woman, they'd railed and screamed at him, and one had even tossed a vase at him.

Not Bella, though.

And the icy cold had him more worried than heat would have.

"What are you talking about?" He took a step toward her, but she shoved her hand out again as if trying to use telekinesis or something to hold him back.

"This," she snapped, reaching into a pocket of her skirt, "I'm talking about *this*." She dragged out a sheet of paper, crumpled it in one fist and then threw it at him.

Jesse snatched it out of the air, scanned it quickly and felt his heart sink. "What the hell?"

"Don't recognize your own handiwork?" she sneered. "Allow me to explain. That is an eviction notice. Giving me three weeks to vacate the property. The property *you* own."

"Bella, you have to know this is a mistake."

"No, I don't. It's all there in black and white," she snapped. Her face was pale and the two bright spots of color on her cheeks stood out in sharp relief. "It's all perfectly clear, Mr. King."

"I'm not evicting you."

"Really?" She tipped her head to one side and glared at him. "Because that paper makes it all pretty official. My lease is up in three weeks and you want me out. All very cut-and-dried."

"I didn't order this—" Jesse broke off, let his head fall back and closed his eyes as he silently cursed his business manager to hell and back.

When he'd first bought Bella's building from the late owner's family, he'd told his business manager to leave her alone until the end of her lease. Well, her lease was up in just a few weeks and apparently, his manager had kept track. Jesse hadn't even *thought* about her damn lease in weeks. Turns out, he should have been paying closer attention.

"Okay, let me explain."

"There is nothing you can say to me that will explain this."

Getting angrier himself by the second, Jesse defended himself. "I told you, this is a mistake. Yes, I admit that eviction plans were drawn up a few months ago, but I told my business manager not to do anything until your lease was almost up—"

"Congratulations, he follows orders exceedingly well."

"I never really planned to evict you, Bella. I wanted a chance to convince you to come on board with my company. And I just…forgot to inform my manager."

"You *forgot?*" Her eyes were wide and horrified. "You *forgot* to tell someone *not* to evict me?"

"Yeah, I grant you, that sounds bad. But in my defense I've been pretty busy the last few weeks. With *you.*"

"So it's my fault." She shook her head in amazement.

"Okay, calm down, Bella. We can talk about this, straighten it all out." He walked toward her again, but stopped when she snarled at him.

"If you touch me now, I swear to God, I'll get violent."

Judging by the look in her eyes, he believed her. A wise man knew when to back off. So Jesse stopped stock-still and met her gaze squarely. "I've said it a million times now. This is a mistake, Bella. You can't believe I'd want you thrown out of your store."

"Why wouldn't I?"

"Dammit Bella, I…*care* about you."

"Don't choke on the words," she told him.

This was not going well. He should have known. Should have kept a closer watch on his business manager, but he'd had so many balls in the air lately, it hadn't been easy keeping an eye on everything. Which she would never accept as an explanation, and he didn't blame her.

He reached up, grabbed his hair with both hands and gave it a yank out of pure frustration. "This doesn't make sense. Think about it. Hell, you just agreed to join my company, why would I do this to you now?"

She laughed shortly, but there was no humor in it and her eyes only gleamed darker. "That, I grant you was a mistake. You messed up there, didn't you? You should have had me sign the papers before you sent your little man with his eviction notice. Bad move there, Mr. Corporate Raider."

"Are we back to that now? I thought we were past that. I thought we understood each other."

"I thought a lot of things, too," she told him. "I thought you were more than you seemed. That there was a heart in there somewhere. But it looks like we both made mistakes."

"Bella—" She was still coldly furious and that worried him. If she were yelling or shouting or calling him names, Jesse thought, he'd have more of a chance of reaching her. As it was, the ice in her eyes made it plain that she wasn't going to listen to a thing he said.

But he was certainly going to try.

Hell, he cared about her. A lot. Maybe more than cared. Maybe it was love. Maybe he'd fallen in love and hadn't even realized it until it was too late.

Jesse staggered. God. He really was an idiot. Was he really going to lose her just when he realized how much he needed her? No way. No way was he going to let her walk away from him now. He had to tell her. Say the words he'd never said to anyone before. Then she'd believe him. She had to.

"Bella, I love you."

She blinked and then choked out a laugh. "Getting desperate are we? Pulling out the big guns?"

Not the response he'd hoped for. Or the one he'd been counting on. "Dammit, I mean it. You're the only woman I've ever said that to."

"And I'm supposed to believe that, right?"

"Yes!" How could she not believe him? How could she not see that she was killing him?

"Well, I don't," she said, her voice even lower now. "Why should I? I agreed to join King Beach and you disappeared. I haven't seen you in days. Because you'd gotten what you wanted."

"That wasn't it," he said, wishing to hell he knew a way to get out of this mess. That he knew what words to say to convince her. "I was thinking. About us. Our…future."

She gave that short, sad laugh again and it tore at something deep inside him. "We don't have a future, Jesse. We never did. All we ever had was a night on the beach three years ago. Because all the rest of it," she added, her voice dropping now to a husky whisper, "wasn't real. These last few weeks. The time we've been together, it was all an act."

"No." He lifted his chin, met her stormy eyes and willed her to believe.

She didn't.

"All the romance," she said. "The seduction. The lovemaking, the laughter. All of it. You never wanted me. You wanted my business. It was all a game."

He felt the sharp slap of shame and hated the feeling.

He'd dreaded this moment, had hoped to avoid it. Would give anything to be able to tell her she was wrong. But he wouldn't win her now by lying.

"That's how it started, yeah," he admitted, and watched the resulting pain flash in her eyes. He felt like the bastard she'd called him. "I heard Nick Acona was after your business, and—"

"So you deliberately came after me to best your friend?"

"That was part of it…" he hedged.

"All of it," she corrected.

"But that's not how it is now."

"Sure," she said with a short nod. Her mouth twisted and pain shimmered in the depths of her eyes. "I believe you. It wasn't a game. And I believe you love me. Why not?"

"Bella, dammit." He took one step toward her and stopped. If he got too close, he'd reach for her and it would kill him if she wouldn't let him touch her. His heart ached, his throat was tight and dry and Jesse felt as if he were fighting for his life. And losing.

He shoved one hand through his hair again and wished for the right words. Finally though, he simply had to start. "I admit I started seeing you in the beginning because I wanted your business. I wanted to beat Nick out. But I wanted you again, too. You haunted me for three years!"

Her mouth worked, but she didn't say anything, she just stood there, watching him, and Jesse felt like a bug under a microscope.

"Everything changed. So damn fast." He laughed a little, shook his head and scrubbed one hand across the back of his neck. "Hell, Bella, I stopped thinking about just your business weeks ago. And I forgot about the blasted eviction notice because I was spending so much time with you, nothing else mattered."

Her expression stayed blank. The hurt remained in her eyes. "I don't believe you."

"I know." He took the eviction notice and ripped it in half. Then ripped those halves again. Tossing them to the floor, he said quietly, "Forget about this, Bella. Stay in the damn shop. Stay rent-free! And forget about King Beach taking over Bella's Beachwear. I don't want your business. I just want you. I don't want to lose you."

"You already have." Bella looked at him and felt her heart break. Nothing he said now could change the fact that he had deliberately set out to seduce her business out from under her. How could she ever trust that he was telling her the truth?

Pain was so sharp and thick inside her that she could hardly draw a breath. He'd said *I love you.* And just hours ago, she would have given anything to hear those words from him. Now it was too late. Now he used those words too easily in an attempt to gloss over what he'd done.

She'd lost everything.

In one fell swoop, it was all gone. Dreams. Hopes. A future with the man she loved. It was all dust, blowing out to sea.

"Besides, I was never really yours to lose," she whispered, realizing the stark truth.

"I don't accept that," he told her and in his blue eyes, she read a determination to fight.

Well, it was too late for that.

"You have to accept it, Jesse," she said, shaking her head and backing away from him. Her fury was gone. The righteous indignation that had spurred her to come here to witness the destruction of everything she cared about had faded away. All that was left now was the pain.

Stepping back from him was the hardest thing she'd ever had to do, but if she didn't pull away now, she'd never be able to live with herself. "It's over. All of it."

"Bella, if you'll just listen—"

"No." She headed for the door, never taking her eyes off him. "I'll move out of the shop. I'll be gone before the end of the month."

"I don't give a damn about that shop. You don't *have* to move out," he snapped.

"Yes, I do." Her hand closed around the doorknob. She glanced back at him over her shoulder and knew she'd keep this picture of him in her mind always. Backlit by the sun glancing off the ocean behind him, his hair was golden, his eyes in shadow and his jaw tight and hard.

Everything in her wanted to run to him, throw her arms around him and pretend for one more day that what they'd shared was real. That what she felt was reciprocated. That, for once, she had someone who loved her.

But if it wasn't real, then none of it mattered.

Sighing, she told him, "You won't be getting my

business. Because *I* am my business and you'll never have me. You don't deserve me, Jesse."

His features tightened and his body flinched as if she'd struck him a physical blow.

"Bella," he said softly, "give us a chance. Give me a chance."

"No more chances. I should have known this was how it would end," she said sadly. "You've never made a commitment to anything in your life. I get that now. And I know that's why you would never commit to me."

"You're wrong," he argued. "I've made plenty of commitments and if you'd just listen—"

She interrupted him. "Jesse, you drifted into owning your company. You hired someone else to build your 'green' house. All you had to do was show up and live in it. You pay someone to recycle your trash. You pay people to run the Save the Waves foundation. Don't you get it? You hire people to make commitments for you, so you never have to bother." She shook her head. "That's not how I want to live my life."

"Bella, don't go." Three words that sounded as though they'd been forced from his throat.

It was too little, too late.

"If it helps, I won't be signing with Nick Acona, either."

"Bella…"

"Goodbye, Jesse." She opened the door, left the office and closed it behind her with a quiet snick of sound.

Two days later, Jesse was still stunned.

No one had ever told him off the way Bella had.

No one had ever been so right about him.

He'd wanted to argue with her, to refute everything she'd said to him, but she'd pegged him perfectly.

He *had* gone through life looking for the easiest route. He'd stumbled into a business that suited him, and only when it was placed right in front of him had he made the effort to grow it successfully. He *did* take a backseat in the running of his ocean foundation. He'd found good people to run it, then salved his conscience by writing hefty checks.

And damn it, she was right about something else, too. He *could* put two trashcans into every cubicle at the office. The janitorial staff would probably thank him profusely for making that job a little easier.

It was a hell of a thing when you got a wake-up call from the woman you loved and she was telling you that you didn't deserve her.

Even worse, he thought, when she was right.

Bella had made him take a good, hard look at himself and Jesse hadn't liked what he'd seen. He'd wanted to go to her house that night. To face her down, admit that everything she'd said to him was right on the money. To even, as hard as it was to swallow, beg her to hear him out. But he'd known that she would still be way too furious to listen to anything he had to say. And who could blame her?

So he'd given it a couple of days. Time enough for that icy temper of hers to thaw a little. Time enough for him to come up with at least a half-baked plan he hoped would work to convince her to come back to him.

A cold sea wind was blasting in off the ocean when

he left King Beach to walk the short block to Bella's shop. Dark clouds studded the sky and seabirds were headed inland. A sure sign that the storm that had been building for days was finally coming in for a landing. Good, he thought. A storm would clear the air and maybe, he told himself, that's just what he and Bella needed, too.

Taking a deep breath of the cold air, he headed for Bella's, walked up to the front door and—it was locked. Scowling, he thought for a second that she'd gone to lunch or something. But it was three in the afternoon, so that wouldn't wash. Cupping one hand over his eyes, he leaned in close to the window and peered inside.

The shop was empty.

Everything was gone. The swimsuit racks stood naked, the cash register was gone from the counter. The walls had been stripped of the swimsuits and posters Bella had had hanging there. Panic rose up in his chest. Not really believing what he was seeing, Jesse moved to another window, one that afforded a peek into the back of the shop, but he didn't feel any better once he checked that one out, too.

Her supplies of fabric were gone. Her worktable was bare and the boxes of new inventory were missing. The entire shop was vacant and as he stood there, locked out on the sidewalk, Jesse felt as empty as the building in front of him.

But damn if he was going to stay that way.

He went back to King Beach, got his car and drove to her house. The tidy flowerbeds, the small patch of lawn, the bright red front door all called to him, made him remember days and nights with her. Memories he didn't want to give up. Promises of a future he didn't want to lose.

He stalked up the front walk, pounded on that red door and waited for a response that didn't come. Looking into the windows, he sighed in relief when he noted that her things were still here, at least. She hadn't skipped town on him. Not that that would have stopped him. It just would have taken him longer to find her.

"Bella!" he called, pounding on the door again. "Bella, open up and talk to me, dammit!"

He waited what seemed like several lifetimes, but she never came to the door. He glanced next door at her friend Kevin's house, but the place was dark and there were no cars in the driveway, so she wasn't hiding out with him. Where the hell was she? Sitting in the living room, listening to him make an ass of himself?

Desperation clawing at his insides, Jesse shouted, "Fine! I'll just sit here on your porch until you come out!"

He spent the next few hours doing just that. He waved at the neighbors, ordered a pizza when he got hungry and he was still sitting there late that night when the brewing storm finally blew into Morgan Beach.

Eleven

The following afternoon, Jesse went to Kevin's shop, determined to get the man to tell him where Bella was. If anyone knew, her best friend would. He pushed the door open and stopped dead.

There was Kevin, with a tall, leggy blonde wrapped around him like shrink-wrap on a DVD. Their kiss was steamy enough to fog up the windows and only ended reluctantly when they heard Jesse's entrance.

The blonde glanced at him, then tucked her face into Kevin's chest on a laugh. "Oops."

Kevin only grinned. "It's okay, Trace. Jesse, this is my girlfriend, Traci Bennett. Traci, Jesse King."

She looked at him and Jesse realized that he recognized her. Her face was in dozens of magazine ads. She was tall, beautiful and dressed in quiet elegance, and all he could think was that he wished he were looking at a short, badly dressed, curvy brunette.

"You're the ex-surfer who's been rebuilding around here," Traci said. "Good job, by the way. Love what you've done to the place."

"Thanks." She liked it. Bella hated it.

"It's nice to meet you," she said. "Um, sorry about your walking in on the kiss, but I've been gone four weeks, and I really missed Kevin."

"No problem," Jesse said, stuffing his hands into the pockets of his slacks. If he could have had his way, he'd be with Bella right now, doing the same damn thing. "I just need to talk to him for a few minutes, if you don't mind."

"Not at all." She reached up, rubbed lipstick off Kevin's smiling mouth with her thumb, then turned and picked up her purse off the counter. "I'll let you guys talk. I'll see you later at my place, honey?"

Kevin's eyes gleamed. "Oh, yeah."

She was gone a moment later, leaving a trail of expensive perfume behind her. Jesse looked at Kevin. "So, you really do have a girlfriend."

"I really do. But is that what you came to talk to me about?" he asked, folding his arms over his chest and giving Jesse the kind of hard stare reserved for bad dogs and crazed children.

Apparently, Bella'd already talked over the situation with her friend and it was no surprise whose side Kevin was on. Fine. He could take whatever the guy had to say.

Hell, he deserved it. But Jesse wasn't leaving here without knowing how to find Bella.

"No, it's not *your* girlfriend I'm worried about," he admitted.

"What I thought." Kevin nodded toward the front door. "Flip the closed sign then come to the back."

Jesse did as Kevin asked, locked the front door, then followed Kevin into what looked like a miniwarehouse. The walls were crowded with shelves filled with boxes and gift wrap and ribbon and more jewelry than one person could use in several lifetimes.

There was also a small sink, a refrigerator, a tiny table and two chairs. Kevin pointed at the table, said, "Take a seat," and turned for the fridge. "Beer?"

"Sure."

Once they were both seated and Kevin had had a sip of his beer, he asked, "So, why are you looking for Bella?"

"Why?" Jesse just stared at him. "Because I have to talk to her."

"Seems to me you guys said everything that needed saying."

"She told you."

"She did." Kevin took another pull at his beer, then set the bottle down on the table, leaned back in his chair and glared at Jesse. "She cried."

"Dammit." He hadn't thought it possible to feel worse than he had been feeling, but he'd been wrong. He hated knowing that she'd cried. Hated even more knowing that he'd caused her tears. "She moved out of her shop."

"You evicted her."

Jesse groaned. "No, I didn't. I tore up the notice. Told her she could stay." Why was nobody listening to him?

"And you think she'd stay after that?"

"No, not Bella," Jesse whispered. "She's got too much pride for that. And she's too hardheaded."

Kevin laughed. "That sounds like pot and kettle talk."

"What the hell does she want from me?" Jesse demanded, unamused and feeling just a little desperate. The longer he went without talking to her, the worse his chances of fixing this were.

"Seems like she doesn't want anything from you," Kevin said thoughtfully.

Jesse cupped the cold beer bottle between his palms and felt the iciness creep inside him. But there was nothing different about that for him. He'd felt cold to the bone for days now. Without Bella…

"She left her shop," he said softly. "She's not at her house and when I call her cell, I get dumped into voice mail instantly."

Kevin sighed and picked up his beer for another sip. "She doesn't want to talk to you, man. She wants you to leave her alone."

"No, she doesn't," Jesse insisted, his gaze spearing into Kevin's. "She loves me."

"She did."

Jesse snorted. "What? She's stopped? Just like that? Turned it off and moved on?"

Kevin shook his head. "Why'd you come to me if you don't want to hear what I'm telling you?"

"I didn't come here looking for advice," he muttered. "I came here looking for Bella."

"She's not here."

"Yeah," Jesse told him with a hard look. "I can see that. So where is she?"

"Now why would I tell you that?" Kevin wondered aloud. "You already broke her heart."

Jesse winced. It hadn't been easy coming to Bella's friend. But whether he wanted to admit it or not, he needed help. He had to find her. Talk to her. Convince her to come back to him. Convince her to take a chance. And if anyone would know where she was, it was Kevin.

Jesse could just admit to the man that he loved Bella. But that was private. Between the two of them. He'd tell her. Again and again until she believed him. But damn if he'd tell her best friend. "I have to talk to her."

"And tell her what?"

"Everything."

"Didn't go so well for you the last time," Kevin said.

"No," Jesse admitted. "She didn't exactly give me a chance, though. She came into the office, reamed me out, then disappeared."

Kevin smiled, took a sip of his beer and said, "So what are you going to do about it?"

"Apparently," Jesse told him, "I'm going to sit in the back room of her friend's shop and be tortured."

"Besides that, I mean."

"I'm going to find her." Jesse glared at him again. "Even if you don't tell me where she is, I'll find her.

Then I'll tie her to a chair if I have to, to make sure she listens to me. Then I'm going to tell her that she loves me and that we're damn well getting married."

"I'd almost like to see that," Kevin mused.

"Enjoying this, are you?"

"Not as much I thought I would." Kevin leaned forward, bracing his arms on the table. "I told you before, that Bella's family to me. You hurt her badly, twice, but I'm willing to give you another chance because I know she's nuts about you."

Hope leaped up in Jesse's chest.

"But," Kevin added, his eyes steely, his features grim, "I'm warning you now. You hurt her again and I'll find a way to hurt you back."

"Understood." It was a measure of just how far gone he was that Jesse was willing to accept that threat from Kevin without batting an eye. Ordinarily, nobody told Jesse King what to do or how to do it. But as Bella's only "family," Jesse figured Kevin was within his rights.

The other man studied him for a long moment or two, then nodded and said, "All right. She's been staying at my place, but she went back home this morning."

"Thanks." Jesse jumped to his feet and headed for the front door.

An hour later, Bella was curled up on her couch feeling sorry for herself when a knock at the door sounded. Her head snapped up. She knew without even looking out the window that it was Jesse. She seemed to be able to sense his presence. Even when she didn't want to.

But she couldn't hide from him forever. She'd had a couple of days to cry and wallow in her misery. Now it was time to reclaim her life. This was her house. Her hometown. And she wasn't going to give it up because she'd made the mistake of loving a man who was incapable of loving her back.

She ran her fingers under her eyes, wiping away any stray teardrops, then checked her reflection in the closest mirror. Her hair was a mess, she wasn't wearing makeup and she looked like exactly what she was. A woman who'd spent too much time lately crying.

He knocked again, louder this time and Bella steeled herself as she opened the door. Her heart squeezed in her chest. He looked so good and she'd missed him so much.

"Bella," he whispered, a relieved smile creasing his features. "Thank God. I've been looking for you for days."

"What do you want, Jesse?" she asked, hugging the edge of the door close, positioning herself across the entryway so he couldn't slip into the house.

He inhaled sharply, blew the breath out in a rush and nodded. "Right. Okay. There's a lot I want to talk to you about, but let's start with this." He held out a sheaf of papers.

She sighed, took them and glanced at the bold, black letters across the top. *Deed.* "What?"

"It's the deed to your building, Bella," he said quickly, giving her that half smile she loved so much. "I want you to have it. Do whatever you want with it. Expand your business or close it. It's yours. No strings."

She looked down at the paper in her hand, then lifted her gaze to his beautiful blue eyes. Shaking her head, she said, "Don't you get it, Jesse? I don't want this. I don't want anything from you." She threw the deed over his head and watched it flutter in the wind until it landed on her lawn. "Now, please. Just go away."

She closed the door on him and tried not to remember the stunned surprise flickering in his gaze. Then she leaned back against the door and let the tears fall again. She'd thought she was finished crying, but apparently, there were more tears locked inside.

He didn't understand. This wasn't about her shop. Her business. Or King Beach. This was about *them*. This was about how she loved him and how wrong she'd been.

"Bella," he said, his voice coming through the door clearly, "don't do this."

She held her breath, closed her eyes and waited him out. Finally, she heard his footsteps as he left the porch and took the steps. When she didn't hear anything else, she slowly sank to the floor, hugged her knees to her chest and sat there silently until she heard him turn and walk away. She'd done the right thing, Bella knew. She had to be strong. She couldn't let herself be hurt again. She just didn't think she would survive another broken heart.

Turning him away was the only thing she could do. Right now, he was reacting to having lost her. He'd already told her that Kings didn't lose, so naturally, he wouldn't give up easily. But eventually, if she stayed strong enough, he'd give up and go away.

Bright and early the next morning though, he was back, pounding on her front door. "Bella! Bella, open up! Talk to me, dammit."

She staggered from bed in the semidarkness of the night just as dawn broke. She hadn't planned to answer the door if he came back. Wouldn't have actually, if he hadn't kept shouting her name so loudly. If she didn't open her door, Mrs. Clayton next door would be calling the police in a few minutes.

Clutching her pale pink robe to her chest, she threw the door open. Cold wind scuttled past her and sent a chill zipping through her body. The sky behind him was a pale violet and studded with dark clouds. The sun hadn't risen yet, but it was close.

Jesse looked as if he hadn't slept. His hair was wild, as if he'd been driving his fingers through it all night. His white shirt was wrinkled, there was a day's growth of whiskers on his jaw and his eyes were shadowed. He held a latte from the diner in each hand. "I brought you coffee."

She sighed, reached out and took one. Fine. He knew her weakness. But that didn't mean anything. Nor did the fact that she'd accepted the coffee.

"Jesse, you have to stop."

"No, I don't," he told her, stepping in close. "I won't stop. Not until you hear me out."

Bella sighed again, heavier this time. He looked as bad as she felt. Why drag this on for either of them? Wouldn't it be easier to just let him say what he felt that he had to say? Then maybe he'd go away. "Okay, talk."

He blinked at her. "Can't I come in?"

"No."

He huffed out a breath, muttered something she didn't quite catch and let his head fall back. "Fine. You don't want me in your house, I'll just say it right here." His gaze met hers. "Bella, I *love* you."

Her breath caught. How amazing that pain could just keep growing. "Jesse…don't…"

"I do." He reached out and when she would have shut the door, he slapped one hand against it, preventing her from closing herself off from him again. "Look, I know I screwed up. I know you're hurt. And pissed. And you've got every right to be. But dammit, Bella, I've never felt this way before. Maybe that's why I'm messing it up so badly. It's all new to me. *You're* new to me. But that doesn't make it less true. I love you, Bella. I really do."

Her throat was closing on her and her vision was blurring. She really didn't want to cry in front of him, but if she didn't get the door closed fast that was exactly what was going to happen and her humiliation would be complete.

His words echoed over and over again in her mind and she wanted to hold on to them. But how could she? She would have given anything to believe him. To hear those words and hold them close. Instead, she said, "How can I believe you, Jesse? You lied to me right from the beginning."

Sorrow glimmered in his eyes and his mouth tightened into a hard, flat line. "I know and I'm sorry. Sorrier than you realize. As I said, I made mistakes. But loving you isn't one of them, Bella. You have to believe me. You have to know that what I feel is real. I want to marry you." He laughed shortly. "There's a sentence I never thought I'd hear myself say."

She shivered and fought to keep her tears from falling. "Stop. Please."

"No," he told her sincerely, his blue eyes fixed on hers, "I'll never stop. You're the soul of me, Bella. You're the piece of me that was always missing. Hell, I didn't even know I was incomplete until I found you." He slid his hand over the door to rest atop hers. "And I can't lose you now. I won't go back to being alone."

Just that one touch of his skin against hers sent heat she hadn't known in days skimming through her system. Still, Bella couldn't believe. Couldn't risk it.

"You were my mystery woman, Bella," he said. "But I see now the only mystery is how I ever managed to live without you in my life. Give me a chance to make it all up to you, Bella. Give *us* that chance."

She stared into his eyes, longing to believe, but just too shattered to try. "I really wish I could believe you, Jesse. But I just can't."

Then she closed the door and let the tears fall.

Late that night, Jesse muttered a curse as the heavens opened up on him. He'd never had to work so hard for anything in his life. Always, things had come easily to him. Always, he'd walked through life, taking what he wanted, leaving the rest behind. Until now.

Now, everything rested on his being able to convince one woman—*the* woman—that she was the most important thing in his world. That she *was* his world.

And he wasn't going to lose.

She was stubborn?

He was more stubborn.

If she thought he was going to give up and go away, then she had a big surprise in store for her. He stepped out of his car and was instantly drenched.

Naturally, it was pouring rain. Wouldn't want this to be easy at all. He stared at Bella's house, glanced at the neighbors on either side. Kevin was probably with Traci and Mrs. Clayton's house was dark. No one would see him. Then he shifted his gaze to Bella's bedroom window. She was in there. Snuggled under her blankets. Alone.

But not for long.

He swiped his wet hair out of his eyes and headed directly across the lawn toward her bedroom. He was through going to the front door, asking her to let him in. Enough already. She was going to listen to him. She was going to *believe* him. And he damn well wasn't going to leave until she did.

He smiled as he lifted her window, glad that it was still unlocked. The last time they'd stayed at her house, he'd noticed that the lock was faulty and had been going to replace it for her. Now he was grateful that he hadn't.

The wood window frame, still soaked from the previous storm, screeched a little as it slid up and Jesse winced. He paused, looked over his shoulder and noticed a light come on in at Mrs. Clayton's. Of course it couldn't have been Kevin who'd heard him. Had to be the neighbor he hadn't met. If she looked out and saw him climbing through a window, she'd be calling the cops any second now.

No time to waste.

He climbed in, hit his shin on the windowsill and muffled the curse that flew from his mouth. On the bed, Bella stirred beneath her blankets and turned so that the dim light of the rainy night fell across her features. Jesse's chest tightened. He loved her more than he'd ever thought it was possible to love anyone.

The room was small and filled with shadows. But he didn't need to see to know where his destination was.

Walking quietly toward the bed, he shrugged out of his jacket and tossed it onto the floor with a sodden splat. Shaking his head, he sat down beside her, laid one hand on her hip and whispered, "Bella. Bella, wake up."

She turned toward him with a slow, languid movement, opened her eyes sleepily and stared up at him. A second passed before she blinked and said, *"Jesse?"*

"Were you expecting someone else?" he asked wryly.

"No, and I wasn't expecting you, either." She scooted back from him, but Jesse wasn't going to lose his momentum now.

He reached out, grabbed her and pulled her to him.

"You're soaking wet!"

"It's raining outside."

"How did you get in here?" She was squirming,

trying to get free of him, but Jesse only tightened his hold on her.

"Climbed through your window." He looked down into her eyes. "You really need to get that latch fixed."

"Apparently."

"Look, Bella, Mrs. Clayton saw me climbing in, I think, so I've gotta talk fast, because she's probably calling the cops to report a break-and-entry."

"Oh, for heaven's sake!"

"You see what I'm willing to do for you?" He asked the question with a wide grin. He was soaking wet, cold down to the bone and yet he hadn't felt so warm in days. Just having her here, beside him, made everything all right. Still smiling, he said, "I'm probably going to get arrested, so now you have to listen to me."

"Jesse, you're crazy."

"Probably."

She swung her hair back from her face and looked up at him, eyes shining. "Why are you doing all this? Why do you keep trying?"

"Because you're worth it," he told her, his voice deep and low. "You're worth anything."

"Jesse, I want to believe you, I really do."

"Because you love me," he said, tracing the pads of his thumbs across her cheekbones. "Why won't you admit it?"

Her eyes closed and a single tear slid from beneath her eyelid. He kissed it away.

"I can't. If I do, you'll break my heart again," she

said, her voice almost lost in the steady patter of the rain falling outside.

Jesse's own heart ached at the misery in her voice and at the knowledge that he'd caused her so much pain. But he could fix that. He would make it his personal mission to see to it that she never cried again.

"No more tears, Bella. You're killing me."

"I can't seem to stop," she admitted, lifting her gaze to look at him again.

"God, I love you so much." He cupped her face in his palms and let his gaze move over her features hungrily. Like a man starved and finally given a feast, he couldn't seem to get his fill of her. "I swear I'll never make you cry again."

She actually laughed at that. "Oh, Jesse, you can't make that kind of promise."

The tightness in his chest eased a little. She wasn't trying to escape from him anymore. She wasn't trying to push him away. That was a start, anyway.

"I will promise it, though." He met her gaze and held it. "Believe me, Bella. I will spend the rest of my life trying to make you smile. Making sure you never doubt again how much I love you."

She chewed at her bottom lip and drew one shaky breath.

Reaching into his slacks pocket, he pulled out the box he'd been carrying all day. He'd gone shopping at Kevin's place that morning right after he left Bella. He flipped the red velvet lid back, displaying the ring that had made him think of Bella the moment he saw it.

"Jesse…"

He reached for her left hand and though she was trembling slightly, she didn't pull away. Slowly, he slid the ring onto her finger and held it in place while they both stared down at it, shining in the darkness.

"It's a yellow diamond," he said, "and when I saw it at Kevin's I thought of you. Those yellow shirts you wear. The way you love the sun. The brightness I feel in the world when I'm with you."

She lifted her free hand and covered her mouth while her eyes drenched and spilled over.

"Now see, I've already broken my promise and made you cry again," he whispered, leaning in to kiss her forehead with a gentle reverence.

"Doesn't count," she whispered. "Tears of happiness don't count."

He smiled and relief washed over him. He was forgiven.

"I love you, Bella. I want to marry you. Have babies with you. Build a life together."

She pulled in another shuddering breath, lifted her gaze to his and said, "I want that, too, Jesse. I love you so much."

"Finally," he said, a wide grin on his face. "You're going to have to say that a lot, you know. Don't think I'll ever get tired of hearing it."

"I can do that," she said.

Taking both of her hands in his, he said, "I'm making a commitment, Bella. To you. To us. I even put recycling cans in the cubicles at the office."

She laughed then, a delightful sound that rippled out around him and settled over Jesse like a blessing.

"Oh, Jesse, you really are crazy, aren't you?"

"Crazy about you? Oh, yeah, baby. Count on it."

Outside, flashing red-and-yellow lights lit up the darkness and Jesse grimaced. "That'll be the police. Honey, would you mind coming out and explaining to the nice officers that this is just the beginning of our very interesting lives?"

Epilogue

Three months later, Bella burst from her office into Jesse's, a wide grin on her face as she waved a sheet of paper in the air as if she were waving the winner's flag at a car race.

"It's here! And it's wonderful! *You're* wonderful!" She flung herself at him and Jesse jumped up from his chair to catch her, arms coming around her in a tight embrace.

His wife.

He didn't think he'd ever get tired of the sound of those two words. *His wife.* He and Bella had been married for a month now and the difference in his life was staggering. He felt more alive than he ever had and it was all because of her.

"What's here and just how wonderful am I?" he asked, bending his head to nibble at her neck.

Since Bella's office was right next to his now, there was a connecting door the two of them alone used. That way they could be together whenever they wanted and without the rest of the office giving them knowing winks and smiles.

Not that he minded.

Bella hummed low in her throat as his lips and tongue moved over her neck. He loved the way she was dressing these days. Jeans that clung to her amazing legs, shirts that were actually her size and usually with nicely scooped out necklines, giving him much easier access.

"That's not fair," she whispered. "You know I can't think straight when you do that."

"Good," he murmured. "No thinking required."

And with the new rules of the office—no one entered without knocking and receiving a response—they were free to do whatever they liked. Jesse smiled to himself. There were several things he could think of to occupy them both for at least an hour or two.

"Jesse…" she squirmed in his grasp. "I didn't come in here for this. I just wanted to show you. To thank you…"

"Ooh, good. I love being thanked by my wife."

She laughed and tossed the paper she'd been holding onto his desk so that she could wrap both arms around his neck. She kissed him then, long and deep, and then pulled back to look up at him. "You say that a lot, you know? *My wife.*"

He grinned at her. "Get used to it. My wife. *Mine.*"

"Just the way I like it," she whispered, and kissed him again, giving him everything he could ever have wanted. Making every dream come true. Making his life just as it should be.

And when she stepped away from him, backing toward the office sofa with a secretive smile, he followed willingly. But first, he glanced at the paper she'd brought into the office and he smiled.

It was the new national ad for King Beach.

Good to know she approved.

The glossy paper carried their pictures, shots of their beachwear and the slogan *Bella and the King. Together at Last.*

It was perfect.

* * * * *

COMING NEXT MONTH

Available October 13, 2009

#1969 MILLIONAIRE IN COMMAND—Catherine Mann
Man of the Month
This air force captain gets a welcome-home surprise: a pretty stranger caring for a baby with an unquestionable family resemblance—to him! Yet once they marry to secure the child's future, will he want to let his new wife leave his bed?

#1970 THE OILMAN'S BABY BARGAIN—Michelle Celmer
Texas Cattleman's Club: Maverick County Millionaires
Falling for the sexy heiress was unexpected—but not as unexpected as her pregnancy! Though the marriage would be for business, their bedroom deals soon became purely pleasure.

#1971 CLAIMING KING'S BABY—Maureen Child
Kings of California
Their differences over children—she wanted them, he didn't—had this couple on the brink of divorce. Now his wife has come back to his ranch…with their infant son.

#1972 THE BILLIONAIRE'S UNEXPECTED HEIR—Kathie DeNosky
The Illegitimate Heirs
The terms of his inheritance bring this sexy playboy attorney a whole new set of responsibilities…including fatherhood!

#1973 BEDDING THE SECRET HEIRESS—Emilie Rose
The Hightower Affairs
When he hires an heiress as his private pilot, he's determined to find proof she's after a friend's family money. Each suspects the other of having ulterior motives, though neither expected the sparks that fly between them at thirty thousand feet!

#1974 HIS VIENNA CHRISTMAS BRIDE—Jan Colley
Posing as the fiancé of his brother's P.A., the playboy financier is happy to reap the benefits between the sheets…until secrets and a family feud threaten everyone's plans.

SDCNMBPA0909